SHE REMEMBERED THE FEEL OF HIM ALL TOO WELL . . .

He bent his head and began to kiss her, a deep, slow, profoundly erotic kiss. She lay back in his arms, her head against his shoulder, her arm coming up to circle his neck. His hand slid down to cup her breast. And the loving touch of his mouth, his hand, shattered what resistance she had left. She felt him as a flame of desire, a flame which burned deep within her; and deep within her rose the urge to answer him, to satisfy him, to give to him and hold back nothing . . .

D1569997

JOAN WOLF is a native of New York City who presently resides in Milford, Connecticut, with her husband and two children. She taught high school English in New York for nine years and took up writing when she retired to rear a family.

Dear Reader:

Signet has always been known for its consistently fine individual romances, and now we are proud to introduce a provocative new line of contemporary romances, RAPTURE ROMANCE. While maintaining our high editorial standards, RAPTURE ROMANCE will explore all the possibilities that exist when today's men and women fall in love. Mutual respect, gentle affection, raging passion, tormenting jealousy, overwhelming desire, and finally, pure rapture—the moods of romance will be vividly presented in the kind of sensual yet always tasteful detail that makes a fantasy real. We are very enthusiastic about RAPTURE ROMANCE, and we hope that you will enjoy reading these novels as much as we enjoy finding and publishing them for you!

In fact, please let us know what you do think—we love to hear from our readers, and what you tell us about your likes and dislikes is taken seriously. We have enclosed a questionnaire with some of our own queries at the back of this book. Please take a few minutes to fill it out, or if you prefer, write us directly at the address below.

And don't forget that your favorite RAPTURE ROMANCE authors need your encouragement; although we can't give out addresses, we will be happy to forward any mail.

We look forward to hearing from you!

Robin Grunder
RAPTURE ROMANCE
New American Library
1633 Broadway
New York, NY 10019

SUMMER STORM

by

Joan Wolf

RAPTURE ROMANCE
NEW AMERICAN LIBRARY
TIMES MIRROR

PUBLISHER'S NOTE

This novel is a work of fiction. Names, characters, places, and incidents are either the product of the author's imagination or are used fictitiously, and any resemblance to actual persons, living or dead, events, or locales is entirely coincidental.

SIGNET, SIGNET CLASSICS, MENTOR, PLUME, MERIDIAN AND NAL BOOKS are published by The New American Library, Inc., 1633 Broadway, New York, New York 10019

First Printing, March, 1983

1 2 3 4 5 6 7 8 9

PRINTED IN THE UNITED STATES OF AMERICA

Chapter One

❦

It was a beautiful day in early May when Mary O'Connor came out of the heavy oak door of the university's Freemont Hall. She paused for a minute on the top of the steps and surveyed the scene below her. The green lawns of the New England campus were heavily speckled with students in various states of undress, reclining under the dogwood trees and cramming for final exams. Mary turned her own face briefly upward to feel the warmth of the sun and someone behind her said, "Dr. O'Connor?"

Mary turned, recognized the student, and repressed a sigh. He was a very large, very amiable, not very clever young man who had, for reasons she could not fathom, decided to fall crashingly in love with her. Considering the fact that the highest mark she had given him all semester was a C, his devotion was a mystery to her.

It was not a mystery, however, to Bob Fowler (the large student) or, indeed, to at least a dozen other

1

men, both young and old, who had come in contact with Mary Catherine O'Connor during the year she had been teaching at this university. It was not, regrettably, her Ph.D. in literature or the impressive scholarly reputation she had acquired upon the publication of her book last year that was the cause of all this male admiration. Rather it was the fact that she was twenty-six years old and beautiful.

As she stood now, poised on the top of Freemont Hall's steps, male heads in the area swung around instinctively. It was an attention Mary scarcely noticed, she was so accustomed to it. She stood listening to Bob Fowler for a few minutes with exemplary patience, shook her head in refusal of his offer to carry her briefcase to her car for her, turned resolutely away from him and started down the steps.

There was a blinding flash of light and instinctively she stopped and looked toward its source. There was a photographer standing at the bottom of the steps and as she looked at him the camera flashed again, twice. "Who are you?" Mary demanded.

"Mary O'Connor? *Doctor* Mary O'Connor?" the photographer answered crisply with a question of his own.

"Yes, but . . ."

"Thank you, doctor." The man sent her a smile and turned to climb back into his car. She hesitated, then shrugged her slim shoulders and watched him drive off. It was probably someone from the campus newspaper, she decided.

Ten days later Mary was once again coming out of Freemont Hall where she had her office. It was an extremely warm day and she was wearing the jacket of her beige poplin suit slung casually over one shoulder in order to get the cooling benefit of her short-sleeved navy polka-dot blouse. There were several students clustered on the stone landing outside the building and they were all talking in excited whispers.

"I'm dying to go talk to him," Mary heard one girl saying. "I wish I had the nerve."

"But what can he be doing *here*?" said a male voice. "Have you heard anything about a movie being shot on campus?"

Slowly Mary looked down the stairs to the man who was the cause of all this excitement. He was leaning against the hood of a smart red sports car and looking around him casually, as if he owned the place. He seemed entirely unaware of all the watching eyes, entirely at his ease. Mary supposed that when you possessed one of the most famous faces in the world, you got used to being watched. "Damn," she said under her breath.

Bob Fowler looked around and saw her. "Dr. O'Connor," he said enthusiastically, "take a look at who's standing there at the bottom of the stairs. It's Christopher Douglas!"

"So I see," she replied coolly, and once again surveyed the tall slim man leaning against the red car. He was looking off down the campus toward where an impromptu soccer game was going on on one of the lawns and his splendid, arrogant profile was clear as a cameo. As she watched he seemed to lose interest in the game and turned back to the building in front of him, looked up, and saw her. Instantly he pushed himself off the car and stood upright, moving unself-con-

sciously and with all the lithe grace she remembered
so well. He kept his dark eyes on her the whole time
she was descending the stairs, unaware, as was she, of
the breathlessly watching students.

She stopped in front of him and looked up. She had
forgotten how tall he was, but then she had not seen
him in almost four years. "Hello, Kit," she said to her
husband. "What are you doing here?"

He didn't answer for a minute but stood looking
gravely down at her. "You're wearing your hair differently," he finally answered, "but otherwise you haven't
changed."

"Nor have you," she replied, returning his regard.
One forgot, she thought to herself, inwardly not half
so calm as she hoped she appeared on the surface, one
forgot he really looked like this. Extreme, completely
male beauty is a very rare phenomenon, and Christopher Douglas had been blessed with it in abundance.
"What are you doing here?" she repeated, clutching
more tightly at her briefcase.

"I came to see you." The movies, she thought, had
never done justice to his voice. It took the theater to
allow him its proper range. "I had no idea of your
home address," he was going on, "so I tracked you
down here. I have to talk to you, Mary. Something
has come up."

She knew, instantly, why he had come. There was a
very strange feeling in the pit of her stomach as she
said, "I don't live very far from here. Do you want to
follow me home? My car is parked in the faculty
lot—over there." She gestured to an eight-year-old
Buick and he nodded.

"All right. That's your father's old car, isn't it?"

"Yes. Daddy passed it on to me a few years ago." He waited for her to move away before he opened the door of his red car and got in. She backed slowly out of her space, moved into the narrow road that crossed the campus, and drove toward the main gate. The small red sports car followed.

"This is very nice," Kit said as he followed her in the front door of the small white clapboard house.

"I'm only renting it," she answered, putting her briefcase down in the hall and leading him into the living room.

He looked around him slowly, taking in the furnishings. "You've still got the rocker," he said. "And the drop-leaf table." His long fingers caressed the wood of the table lovingly; he had stripped and refinished that table himself.

"Yes." She bent her head, not looking at him. "Can I get you a drink?"

"I'll take a beer, if you've got one." He sat down on the sofa, which was new and held no memories, and stretched his long legs in front of him.

"Yes, I have beer. I keep some in for Daddy when he comes to visit." She walked into the kitchen, hung her jacket over one of the kitchen chairs, and opened the refrigerator. She was annoyed to find her hands were shaking. She opened the beer, got out two glasses and then poured herself a stiff Scotch. She brought his beer into the living room, got her own drink and went to sit in the rocker.

"How *is* your father?" He sipped his beer and regarded her inscrutably over the rim of the glass.

"Fine. He hasn't retired, but at least he isn't accepting new patients anymore. He and mother actually went to Europe for a month earlier this spring." She ran a finger around the rim of her glass. "I think they finally feel they've got me off their hands."

"You landed yourself a very good job," he said, "in a very prestigious university."

She shrugged. "It was about time." She changed the subject. "You're looking very fit. California life must agree with you—you're dark as a gypsy."

"The weather is good," he agreed. He took another sip of beer. "Even you might tan a bit out there."

"Me?" She glanced down at her bare arm. "I doubt it. I've never had a tan in my life. Sunburn now, that's different."

He looked at her for a moment in silence and then said, slowly and deliberately, "I have never seen skin as beautiful as yours."

Damn him, damn him, damn him, she thought. "It's Irish skin," she answered lightly and took a gulp of Scotch.

"Irish eyes too."

She put her glass down with a sharp click and stared at him. "All right, Kit, we've traded compliments and upheld the social amenities. Now perhaps you'll tell me why you came here." She sounded annoyed. "You could have gotten my address from Mother, you know. You didn't have to look me up right on campus, in front of a gaggle of star-struck students. How am I going to explain that?"

"I didn't like to call your mother," he answered a little grimly.

She picked up her glass and took another swallow of Scotch. Better to get it said and done with, she thought. "I imagine you're here about a divorce." Her voice to her own ears sounded hard and flat.

"Is that why you think I've come?"

"I can't imagine any other reason. In fact, I can't imagine why you didn't divorce me years ago."

"I might ask you the same question."

He had the darkest eyes of anyone she had ever known. She found it difficult to keep looking at them and gazed instead at her elegant foot, sensibly shod in a plain navy pump. "I thought I'd leave it to you," she mumbled.

"*You* were the one who threw me over," he replied. "*You* were the one who said you would never live with me again."

"Mmph," she said.

"For an English scholar you're damned inarticulate." His voice sounded distinctly amused.

She glared at him. "I didn't divorce you because a divorce isn't going to make any difference to me. You know that. *I* can't marry again. But you can, so if you want a divorce I'll give you one. I don't believe in being a dog in the manger."

"Do you know, I thought that might be it," he said softly. "So there isn't anyone else?"

"Good God, Kit," she replied irritably, "you know my family. The O'Connors are more Catholic than the pope. No, I'm stuck with the single life." She looked at him challengingly. "And I find it very much to my taste. One marriage was quite enough for me, thank you."

"I see. So you plan to hide yourself away in a cloister for the rest of your life."

"The university is hardly a cloister. And I am not

hiding away. I have work to do. It's the work you are doing that really counts in life—surely you of all people will agree with that."

"I would have—five years ago." His face was still and reserved, quite unreadable. Before she could ask what he meant he went on. "I didn't come to ask you for a divorce."

"You didn't?" He had, as always, thrown her off her balance. "Then what did you come for?" she asked for the third time.

"Was there a photographer around the school last week bothering you?"

Really, she thought, his habit of answering a question with a question was very annoying. "Yes," she said shortly.

"He was from *Personality*."

"What!" *Personality* was the most notorious scandal sheet in the country.

"I'm afraid so," he answered bleakly. "Have you ever seen the paper?"

"I've seen it in the supermarket. I read the headlines while I'm waiting on line."

"Well, your picture will be gracing page one next week," he said. Then, rather inadequately, "Mary, I'm sorry."

She was staring at him in stunned horror. "Are you serious?" He nodded. "I see." She swallowed hard, remembered her Scotch and picked it up. It was empty. "Damn," she said.

"Make yourself another," he suggested.

"No." She shook her head. "Another one of those and I'll be on my ear. Do you want another beer?"

"No."

"All right," she said tensely. "You'd better explain."

He ran a hand through his thick black hair in a gesture that was achingly familiar. "Yes," he said. "That's why I came."

"I don't know how closely you have followed my career," he began slowly, "or if you have followed it at all, but you must have realized that no one in Hollywood knows that I am married."

She had in fact read everything about him that came her way and she had seen all his pictures, but she wasn't going to tell him that. "Certainly, no one has ever disturbed *me*," she replied. "Until now, that is."

"I know. And I didn't want you disturbed, which is precisely why I kept my mouth shut. I don't give many interviews, you know, or go in for talk shows or things like that, so no one has had the opportunity to pin me down on my marital status. Everyone just assumes I'm single."

"You mustn't be terribly popular with the media if you are so unforthcoming," she said lightly.

He smiled, teeth very white in his tanned face. "I'm not." The smile faded. "I learned exactly what the media can do to you when I was making my first picture." There was a note of bitterness in his beautiful voice. "But then you know all about that."

She was staring in fascination at the toe of her shoe. "Yes, I remember."

"So, naturally," he resumed his story evenly, "if a reporter thinks he's got a good bit of gossip about me, he's keen to use it. I don't know how, but someone from *Personality* found out about you."

Her eyes traveled slowly from her toe to his face. "You can't squash it?"

"No. I only found out about it because my cleaning lady's daughter is a typist at the paper. She told me about it yesterday. I thought that the least I could do was warn you."

"How much do they know?" Her voice was barely a whisper.

"Not everything." He leaned forward. "They know we were married and that we split up after all the newspaper gossip about me and Jessica Corbet. That's all."

"Are you sure?" Her lips were white.

"Yes."

"I—see. Do they know we're still technically married?"

"Oh yes, that's the juiciest info of all from their point of view. Christopher Douglas's secret wife and all that rot."

"Oh, Kit, *why*?" she almost wailed. "*Why* did this have to happen?"

"I'm sorry, Mary," he repeated.

"You should have divorced me ages ago," she said. "Why didn't you?"

"Because I didn't want to," he answered coolly. "Like you, I saw no necessity. You are the only woman I have ever wanted to live with permanently."

"You didn't want to live with me" she contradicted him in a low voice. "You just wanted to sleep with me. Unfortunately, you had to marry me to do that." He pushed his hand through his hair once more and she smiled a little at the gesture. "I don't blame you,

Kit, not anymore. I was as much at fault. I shouldn't have married you."

"Well, you did," he said in an odd voice, "and here we are." He looked slowly around the room and his eyes stopped at the overflowing bookcase. "Are you happy, Mary? Do you have what you want?"

"Yes," she answered, ignoring the pain that had unaccountably appeared around her heart. "I've made a place for myself in a world I've always loved. Yes, I'm happy."

"I'm glad. But surely you take a break from academia once in a while? What are you doing this summer? Not more research?"

"No." She lifted her chin proudly. "This summer I've been invited to lecture at Yarborough."

His head came up, poised and alert. "Have you really?"

Yarborough College was a very small school on the shores of a New Hampshire lake. It had, however, over the past ten years acquired considerable national prominence because of its summer dramatics program. The head of the drama department, George Clark, was a bit of a genius, and the small campus theater was a gem of acoustical and dramatic engineering. The combination of the two had produced the Yarborough Summer Festival, in which top drama students from all over the country were given the opportunity to work in a theatrical production with a few noted professionals. Each year the festival did one play and concentrated on one period of theatrical history. A prominent scholar of that period was always invited to lecture and the college gave graduate credit to all the drama students who attended.

"They're doing the English Renaissance this year," she said, "and as you know that's my period. So, for the price of a few lectures, I'll have a lovely New Hampshire vacation."

"What play are they doing?"

"They're being very ambitious. It's *Hamlet.*"

"*Hamlet*? And who is to play the lead?"

"Adrian Saunders," she said, naming a young English actor who had made a hit in a recent British series run on public television.

"Ah." He smiled at her, the famous devastating smile that was calculated to turn every woman's bones to water. "It sounds like fun."

She rose to her feet and he rose also. "I think it will be."

He stood for a moment, looking down at her. "I'm afraid you're going to be bothered, Mary. Just refuse to answer all questions. Don't worry about being polite. Refuse all interviews. It will all die down in a short while, I promise you."

"I suppose so." She sighed and then suddenly became very formal. "Good-bye Kit. It was kind of you to have come." She did not offer him her hand.

"I'm sorry it was on this particular business," he replied gravely. "Do you know, no one has called me Kit for years." He turned and walked swiftly out the door.

She heard his car door slam and the engine start up. In a minute he had backed out of her driveway and had disappeared up the street. Mary sat down in her pine rocker and looked blindly at the sofa where he had sat. She had not felt so upset since the last time they had met.

She would have been even more upset if she had heard the conversation Kit had with his agent early the following day. "Chris!" said Mel Horner genially when his secretary informed him who was on the phone. "What are you doing in New York?"

"Never mind that Mel," Kit replied. "I want you to book me into the Yarborough Festival this summer."

"What!"

"You heard me," Kit replied testily. "I want to work at the Yarborough Festival. They're doing *Hamlet*, with Adrian Saunders."

"But if they have Adrian Saunders for Hamlet, what will you . . ." The agent's voice trailed off in bewilderment.

"I'll play whatever they've got left." His client's voice was clear as a bell over the three-thousand-mile connection. "Laertes, Claudius, the gravedigger—I don't care."

"But Chris," his agent expostulated, "that is exactly the sort of thing you always avoid like the plague. The media will swamp you, wanting to know why you're taking such a small role . . ."

"Goddammit, Mel," Kit said savagely, "I don't want a lecture. I want you to get me into that festival. I don't care what I play, or how much money they offer. I just want *in*. Is that clear?"

"Yeah," said his agent faintly. "I'll get on it right away."

"Good," said Kit, and hung up the phone.

Four days after Kit's visit the storm broke over Mary's head. *Personality* hit the stands with a picture on the cover of her standing on the steps of Freemont Hall. "CHRIS DOUGLAS MARRIED!" screamed the headline. "Wife University Professor!"

"Huh," said Mary when she first saw it. "I wish I *were* a professor." Then her phone started to ring and it didn't stop until the end of the term when she fled the campus and went into seclusion.

She went to Nantucket, where her oldest brother had a summer cottage. Her sister-in-law was in residence with the three children and Mike came out from Boston on weekends. Kathy was a warm and intelligent person who had the tact to leave Mary to herself and not burden her with unwanted sympathy. Mary played tennis with Kathy and went bicycling and swimming with the children. There was no television in the cottage and the only paper Mary saw for two weeks was the local *News*. It should have been a thoroughly relaxing time for her. She was with people she loved and who loved her, and she was doing all the recreational things she liked best to do. It was therefore disconcerting to find herself so restless and dissatisfied.

She knew what was bothering her—more precisely, she knew *who* was bothering her. She had thought she was over him. She had put him out of her life and her work and that, she had thought, was that. She had convinced herself that her happiness lay with things of the mind, not with a dark, slim man who had once torn her life apart and almost destroyed her in the process.

The day before she was due to leave Nantucket for Yarborough it rained. After lunch Mary took an old brown raincoat of Mike's and went for a walk. She went down to the beach and there, with the rain falling on her face and the waves crashing on the sand, she thought back to those innocent undergraduate days of five years ago when she had first met Christopher Douglas.

Chapter Two

She had heard of him long before they met. He was in the graduate drama school at her university in New Haven and had been something of a celebrity on campus for over a year. For one reason or another, Mary had never been to any of the drama productions in which he had starred. She herself was very busy, and in the English department something of a celebrity in her own right. She was, for example, the only undergraduate ever allowed to take the famous graduate seminar of the university's leading professor of Renaissance literature. Mary O'Connor, ran the talk in the English department, had all the marks of a real scholar.

Her commitment to her work scared off a number of boys who would otherwise have wanted to take her out, but she didn't lack for dates. At twenty-one, tall and slender, with long black hair, dazzling pale skin and absolutely blue eyes, she was stunning enough to be forgiven for her brains. She was the youngest of five children and, her brothers and sisters all said affectionately, the smartest. That was why her mother had relented and allowed her to attend a secular, coeducational university. Both her older sisters had gone to a Catholic college for women and upon graduation both had taught school for two years and then married.

"Mary Kate is different," her sister Maureen had told her mother. "For one thing, she's ten years younger than I am and seven years younger than Pat. That's two generations in today's age, Mom. She shouldn't be bound by the same rules we were." And her conservative, apprehensive, but deeply caring mother had relented. Mary had gone to school in New Haven, only a few miles away from her native Connecticut town but worlds away in outlook and philosophy.

She had loved it. And she had not, as her mother had feared, been "corrupted" by bad influences. At the beginning of her senior year she still did not smoke pot or get drunk every weekend; and she was still a virgin.

It was shortly before the Christmas break that a boy she had been dating invited her to see the drama-school production of *Twelfth Night*. "Christopher Douglas is playing Orsino." he told her, "and he's supposed to be terrific."

"Okay," said Mary casually, "I'd like that."

She went, and her whole life changed.

She would never forget the first time she laid eyes on Kit. The lights in the theater had dimmed, the curtain had slowly risen, and there he was, alone in the center of the stage, reclining carelessly against some brightly colored cushions. The first thing she had noticed was his voice. It came across the footlights, effortlessly audible, deep and velvety with just the suspicion of a drawl.

> If music be the food of love, play on,
> Give me excess of it, that, surfeiting,
> The appetite may sicken, and so die.

She listened, breathless, caught in the magic of that voice. Then he rose and moved toward the front of the stage and she really looked at him for the first time. He was a splendid young male, beautiful and tall, slim-hipped and black-haired, with a virility whose impact she felt even across the distance that separated them. She sat rooted to her seat throughout the entire performance. She had never dreamed, she thought, that a boy like this could really exist in the world.

Afterward she and her date, whose name she never afterward remembered, went out for something to eat. They stopped around first to see a friend in one of the dorms, so they were late getting to the local eatery they had made their destination. When they came in the door the place was crowded. Her date had taken her arm and was steering her into the room when someone called his name. They turned and saw a tableful of students eating pizza and drinking beer. One of the students was Christopher Douglas. The boy who had called to them spoke for a minute to her date and then, as they were turning to leave, her escort said to Kit, "We just saw *Twelfth Night*. It was terrific."

"I'm glad you liked it," the beautiful voice replied pleasantly. He looked at Mary and stood up. "Why don't you two join us? I'll round up a few extra chairs."

Before she quite knew what was happening, Mary found herself sitting next to Him. "Did you like the play as well?" he asked her.

"Yes, I did," she answered. "Very much. Your interpretation of Orsino was fascinating."

He raised a black eyebrow. "Oh?"

She subjected him to an appraising blue stare. "If you were even the *slightest* bit effeminate," she said at last, "you couldn't have gotten away with it."

He grinned appreciatively. "Do you know the play?"

"Yes. The English Renaissance is a particular interest of mine."

"Ah. An English major."

Her date caught his last words and leaned across her. "Not just an English major, a summa cum laude English major."

Mary flushed with annoyance. "Perhaps I ought to tattoo it on my forehead in case any one should miss the fact," she said lightly. The remark passed completely over the head of her date but *he* looked at her even harder.

"Hey, Kit," called one of the students from further down the table. "I meant to ask you if you'd seen the latest production at the Long Stage."

"No," he answered, easily pitching his superbly trained voice down the length of the table, "I haven't." A jukebox was playing and a few couples were up in a

small dance area. "Would you like to dance?" he said
to Mary.

"Why, all right," she replied, startled, and he took
her by the hand and led her out to the floor.

"I'm afraid I didn't get your name," he said,
drawing her competently into his arms.

"It's Mary O'Connor. Did I hear someone call you
Kit?"

"Mm." His mouth wore a faint smile. "After Kit
Marlowe, the Elizabethean playwright. Jim thinks I
look the way he must have."

Mary thought of Marlowe, brilliant, poetic, and
dead in a barroom brawl at the age of twenty eight.
She laughed. "He may be right."

He pulled her closer until she could feel the whole
hard length of his body pressed against hers. The
music was slow and dreamy. Mary felt herself relaxing
against him, relaxing into him. "Do you live on campus? Can I take you home?" he murmured into her
ear.

The music stopped and she pulled away from him.
"No, you may not take me home," she said with what
she hoped was firmness. "I came with someone else
and *he* will take me home."

She turned and made her way back to their table.
Her date looked both grateful and relieved when she
sat down and immediately began to talk to him. They
stayed for another thirty minutes during which time
she could feel Kit's dark gaze boring into the back of
her head. When they got up to leave she smiled gener-
ally around the table and refused to meet his eyes.

She thought to herself as she undressed and got into

bed that she had behaved like a child. He must think that no one had ever suggested going home with her before. She should have been funny and casual and made a clever remark. The problem was he unnerved her so much that she *still* couldn't think of a clever remark. She thought of the feel of his body against hers and of her reaction. The problem was, she thought, he scared her to death.

He called the next day and asked her out. She said she was busy. He named another time and she said she was busy then too.

"Doing what?" he asked.

She thought he was being rude and answered repressively, "I'm working on a paper." She would have liked to tell him that what she did was none of his business. She didn't, however, because she was almost constitutionally incapable of being rude herself. Her parents, she thought regretfully, had brought her up too well.

"When is the paper due?" he asked relentlessly.

"The day before Christmas recess. Then I go home." That should give him enough of a hint, she thought.

"I'll call you after the vacation then," said the beautiful voice in her ear and she stared at the phone in astonishment.

"I'll probably be busy preparing for finals," she got out.

"I'll call you," he said firmly and hung up.

She went home for Christmas and tried not to think about Christopher Douglas. She went out with a boy

she had known since high school who was also home
on holiday and she found the dates strangely de-
pressing.

"You don't look very happy, honey," her father
said to her as she came into the living room one night
after saying good-bye to her escort in the car.

"I don't know, Daddy," she replied with a sigh. "It's
just that I'm so *sick* of mediocre boys."

"Mediocre?" he queried with a grin.

"Well, they're nice enough, I guess. It's just that
they don't interest me much. And lately it seems everyone I go out with starts to talk about marriage.
Why do men always want to get married?"

He laughed. "Does Dan want to marry you?"

"I think so," she answered gloomily.

"I always thought you liked Dan."

"Oh, I like him. But he's so—so conventional. His
talk, his ideas, his clothes, his car. I don't think in all
the years I've known him that he's ever once surprised
me."

"Well, then," her father said gravely, "clearly you
oughtn't to marry him."

"No." She sighed. "I don't think I'll ever marry. I
think I'll devote my life to scholarship. It's much more
satisfying than going out on all these boring dates."
She trailed gracefully upstairs, leaving her father with
his head buried in the newspaper, his shoulders shaking.

She got back to college on Monday and by Friday
he still hadn't called. She was unreasonably annoyed.
If people said they were going to do a thing, then they

ought to do it, she thought. She refused two dates for Saturday night and was sitting in her room reading *Tamburlaine the Great* by Christopher Marlowe when she was called to the phone. He was down in the lobby. Would she care to go out with him for a bite to eat?

"All right," she heard herself saying. "I'll be down in five minutes." She brushed her long hair, dusted some blusher on her cheeks and put on lipstick. She changed her jeans for a pair of corduroys, picked up her pea jacket and went downstairs to the lobby.

They had a wonderful time. She had thought they could have nothing in common, but by the end of the evening she felt she had known him forever. She didn't quite know what she had expected—a "film star" type personality, she supposed, to go with his looks. But he wasn't like that at all. He was, in fact, the nicest boy she had ever met. The nicest man, she corrected herself, as she said good night to him sedately in the lobby of her dorm. He was twenty-five, four years older than she, and centuries older in experience she was sure. She did not invite him up to her room.

Mary shivered a little; the Nantucket rain was turning colder and she got up and began to walk slowly down the beach. It was painful, looking back like this; painful to look honestly and see how cocksure and how foolish and how young she had been. And yet she knew, as she reflected on the self-absorbed adolescent she had been, that she could not have handled things any differently from the way she had. Her only alternative had been to simply say good-bye and refuse to see him. And that was something she had not been able to do.

They had reached the crisis point in their relationship rather quickly. He wanted to go to bed with her and she would not. He was very persuasive, and every sense she owned was screaming for her to give in to him, but there was a hidden core of iron in Mary's character and on this issue he came up against it.

"But, Mary, why?" he asked, his lips moving tantalizingly along her throat. They were both in the front seat of a car he had borrowed and the car was parked in front of her dorm. He wanted to come up to her room.

"No, Kit," she said, and his mouth moved to find hers once again. She closed her eyes; nothing she had ever experienced had prepared her for the way she felt when Kit kissed her. His hand slid inside her open coat and began to caress her breast.

"I want you," he said. "I want you so much. Mary—let me come upstairs."

"No," she said again.

"God damn it, why not?" Frustrated passion was making him lose his temper.

She gave him the same answer she had given all the other boys, the answer that had stood her in such good stead for four years. "Because it's a sin," she said and stared resolutely out the front window.

"What?"

That was the answer she usually got. "You heard me. It's a sin. Against the sixth commandment—you know, the one that says, 'Thou shalt not . . .'"

"I know what the sixth commandment says," he replied irritably. He looked at her, trying to make out her expression in the dark. "Are you serious?"

And in fact she was. Then, as now, she was as oddly simple in some ways as she was bafflingly complex in others. Sex before marriage was a sin and she wouldn't do it.

He had tried to change her mind. By God, he had tried. He would have succeeded too, she thought, if she hadn't been so careful about where she would go with him. He was as hampered by lack of opportunity as he was by her own resistance. You can't make passionate love in the middle of a crowded student party—or at least not if you are as private a person as Kit was. You could do quite a few things at a movie, but certainly not what you ultimately wanted to do. He didn't own a car, and on the few occasions when he suggested borrowing one, she had said she had other things to do.

He stopped calling her and for a month she didn't see him. It was pure hell and it was then that she came to the reluctant realization that she loved him. It was a terribly upsetting recognition. They were of two different worlds, really, and she feared and mistrusted his. Those worlds had touched briefly here at college but in June they both would graduate, and like two meteors on opposite courses, they would grow farther and farther apart as the years passed, never to touch each other again. She would continue her studies and, with luck, land a teaching job in a decent university. He would make it big in acting; she had no doubt at all about that. He had the looks, the talent, and the drive. Most of the boys she knew traveled through life in a pleasant cloud; they did things because they seemed like good things to do at the moment. Not Kit. He knew exactly what he was doing and exactly where he was going. And he was going to the top. There was no place for her in the future he envisioned for himself.

In March she learned she had been awarded a fellowship for graduate study. Kit was offered a job with the Long Stage, a regional theater based in New Haven that often sent productions on to Broadway. He called her up to tell her the good news and to congratulate her on her award. Her heart almost jolted out of her body when she heard his voice and she agreed to go out with him for a drink to celebrate.

They went to Guido's, the place where they had first met. Kit ordered a pizza and—as a special treat—a bottle of wine instead of the inevitable beer.

"I've located a small apartment in a decent area of New Haven," he told her, his strong white teeth making quick work of the pizza. "It's in a two-family house. Not very elaborate, but it's clean. And cheap. And I have yard privileges." He looked at her out of brooding dark eyes. "You could move in with me while you're working on your degree."

"No," she said.

"Christ, sometimes I think that's the only word you know."

She put her wineglass down. "You shouldn't have called me up. I shouldn't have come with you." There were tears in her eyes. "I'll get a cab back to my dorm."

"No." His long fingers shot out and closed over her wrist. "No, sit down, Mary."

Slowly she obeyed him and while she fished around in her purse for a tissue he began to talk. "I'm bound and determined to stick to acting. You know that. It's what I want to do most in life. It's what I think I can be *good* at. I have a job at present but the money stinks. I have no family to fall back on if I lose it. I've gone through school on scholarships and loans and my net worth is a debit account."

He looked at her and his flexible mouth was taut and grim. "You don't know what it means to need money. You come from a comfortable New England home. Your father is a doctor and your mother belongs to all the right clubs and committees. Your sisters and brothers are pillars of the community. You have brains and beauty and integrity. You're probably right to run like hell from me. You ought to marry a lawyer or an engineer. Someone like your brothers, who can give you a big house in a nice New England town where you can teach in the local college and raise your kids to play on the local little league team."

She sniffled into her tissue. "You seem to have my life all planned out for me."

He paid no attention to her interruption but went on, his face dark and intense. "My own future is uncertain, to say the least. I have no business asking any girl to tie herself to me—and especially not you." She was looking at him now, her face as somber as his. "But I love you," he said. "This last month has been hell."

"I know." Her words were barely a whisper. "I love

you too." She looked down at his lean hard hand, which was clasped tensely about his wineglass. "Why especially not me?" she asked.

"Because of all the things I've just said. You aren't cut out to be an actor's wife. And for you, marriage would be a serious business."

She kept her eyes on his hand. "Yes." A strand of long black hair had fallen forward across her cheek and she pushed it back behind her ear with a slow, unconsciously seductive gesture.

"So, given all that," he said harshly, "will you marry me?"

With almost palpable effort she dragged her eyes away from his hand and looked up at his face. She moistened her lips with her tongue. "Yes," she said. "I will."

Kit burst upon her quiet, conservative, academically oriented New England family rather like a bombshell. Her mother, obviously worried about the proposed marriage between her youngest daughter and this extraordinary boy, spent a good deal of time during the long weekend they stayed with her family trying to probe Mary's feelings. Mary was certain she was regreting the nice woman's college she had wanted her daughter to attend. Kit would not have come into her orbit if she had been safely cloistered at Mount Saint Mary's.

"You are so *unalike*, darling," she said cautiously to Mary. "You are so intelligent. Learning has always mattered so much to you."

"Kit isn't exactly stupid, mother," Mary replied patiently. "He has a B.S. in mathematics from Penn State, you know."

"Mathematics?" Her mother looked astonished.

"Yes. He got into acting when he joined a student production at Penn for a lark and he ended up deciding he liked it better than math. But he finished his degree. It took him six years to do it, because he had to work, but he finished. He *does* finish what he starts, and he is a very good actor. He'll make it."

"Suppose he does, darling." Her mother's voice was troubled. "Will you like that sort of life? The publicity is ghastly. And I'm sure most of those people in Hollywood take drugs. And the divorce rate . . ."

"I know all that, Mother, and believe me I've thought about it." Mary smiled a little ruefully. "But I love him. What else can I do?"

Her mother's face relaxed a little. "Your father seems to like him," she said hopefully.

Mary grinned. "You know, Mother, I've decided the worst thing you can do is to decide on the sort of man you *don't* want to marry and the sort of life you *don't* want to lead. The minute you do that, God looks down on your smug little plans and says, 'Ah-ha, I'll fix her.' And he did just that. He sent me Kit."

"He is—rather awesome." For the first time there was the hint of laughter in her mother's voice.

"I don't know what he is. I only know that there he is and I've got to be with him."

"Well, then, darling," said her mother briskly, "shall we plan for a wedding in June?"

Kit was rather startled to find that his nuptials were to be celebrated with as much pomp as Mrs.

O'Connor clearly envisioned. But it wasn't the trimmings he objected to so much as the delay.

"June!" He groaned. "Are you going to make me wait until June?"

Mary's eyes always seemed to get at least two shades bluer whenever she looked at him. "Yes, I'm afraid I am."

"But what does it matter, since we're going to be married anyway." His voice had dropped to the husky note that always made her heart begin to race. "What difference can a wedding ring make?" he coaxed.

"It isn't the ring. It's the sacrament," she said patiently. "Oh, Kit, I've explained and explained . . ."

"I know." He had glowered at her dauntingly. "I can't think clearly anymore. And it's all your fault."

She had bit her lip and then giggled. "Darling, you look so funny . . ." And he had stalked off in high dudgeon.

They were married the week after graduation in the church where Mary had been baptized, and there had been a reception for two hundred people on the lawn of the O'Connor family home. They were to go to Cape Cod for their honeymoon, but after they left the reception Kit got on the highway going west rather than east.

"Hey," said Mary in a startled voice. "You're going the wrong way."

"No, I'm not," he replied calmly. "We're going to spend tonight in our own apartment. We can leave for the cape tomorrow."

"Good heavens, why did you decide to do that? We're all booked into the cottage in Chatham."

He gave her a sidelong glance that emphasized the remarkable length of his lashes. "I have no intention of driving five hours on my wedding day," he said. "I'm saving my strength for other things."

It took a minute for his words to register, but when they did she felt a strange shiver deep inside her. "Ah," she got out, she hoped calmly, "I see."

Their apartment consisted of a bedroom, living room, and eat-in kitchen. It was sparsely furnished, mostly from the O'Connor-family attic. The bedroom, however, did boast a double bed with a beautiful maple headboard, and it was to this room that Kit steered her as soon as they were in the door. He put their suitcases down with a thump and went to pull down the shades. When he had performed this task to his satisfaction, he turned to look at his wife.

She was wearing a blue seersucker shirt-dress and sandals. Her long hair, which reached halfway down her back, was tied loosely at the nape of her neck with a blue ribbon. She looked back at him, raised a black eyebrow and said, "Well? Are you going to show me what you've been making such a fuss about for the last six months?"

He tackled her. She was standing next to the bed, and his rush toppled her backward so she was lying on the white Martha Washington bedspread with him on top of her. She began to laugh. He growled and bit her ear. She laughed harder. "I love your subtle technique," she got out breathlessly through her mirth.

"Oh, so you like subtlety?" He slowly pulled the ribbon out of her hair, dropped it on the floor, and bent his head to kiss her. Her mouth opened under his and her arms went up to circle his neck. Always before, she had put a barrier between them, always there had been the awareness that she would let him go so far and no farther. Today the barrier was gone.

When he raised his head and spoke, his voice was husky and his breathing uneven. "And now," he said, "let me see what I've got here." He began to unbutton the front of her shirt-dress. She lay perfectly still, gazing up at him out of darkened eyes. In a minute he had skillfully bared the upper part of her body; her skin was flawless, her breasts perfect. "Almighty God," he muttered. "You're so beautiful." Very gently, almost tentatively, he touched the single small beauty spot that lay near the nipple of her right breast. His light touch sent an electrifying sensation through her entire body.

"Kit," she whispered. "Darling."

He bent to kiss the beauty mark and his hands began to move caressingly on her body. "My princess," he said. "My beautiful Irish witch." He unbuttoned the rest of her dress and then his hands were tugging on the elastic of her half-slip and panties. Instinctively she stiffened and he began to murmur endearments again while his mouth and his hands touched and caressed her. There was extreme tenderness in his voice and in his hands, and sweet cajolery, and the hypnotic quality of rising passion. When Mary's body arched up against his, he released his hold on her only long enough to tear off his own clothes.

She clung to him, swept along on the tide of rising desire. Her brain, that sharp, critical, well-trained arbiter of her life, was swamped by the purely physical sensations Kit's touch aroused. He was murmuring to her and blindly she obeyed his instructions, needing him desperately to assuage the throbbing ache he had created within her. He loomed powerfully over her and she held him tightly, heedless of the pain, stunned by the unexpected searing intensity of the pleasure. He was saying her name over and over; dimly she heard him through the waves of sensation that were sweeping her body. "I love you," she whispered as she felt them coming to rest. "I love you."

They lay still together for a long minute and she ran her hands over the strong muscles of his shoulders and back, feeling the light sheen of sweat that clung to him. His heart was hammering; she could feel the heavy strokes as she felt the heat of his body and the laboring of his breath. She was a little awestruck at the thought that she had been able to do this to him. And when she thought of what he had done to her. . . .

After a while she murmured, "Do you know, this is the first time I've ever understood Anna Karenina?"

He laughed, a soft dark sound deep down in his throat, and raised his head to gaze into her face. The look he gave her was brilliant, full of amusement and triumph. "I hope you're not planning to throw yourself under a train?"

Her lips curved and she felt her heart turn over with love. "You know what I mean." She traced the outline of his mouth. "I never understood what love of a man can do to a woman."

He kissed her fingers and then her throat. "You're so generous, Princess. It's one of the reasons I love you."

They lay quietly together, content and peaceful.

Then Mary whispered, "I ate hardly anything at the reception and I'm starving."

He yawned and sat up. "Great minds think alike. I've just been contemplating calling out for a pizza."

"Yum." She sat up as well. "With sausage."

"With sausage." His eyes narrowed a little as he looked at her. "I warn you, though, the pizza is just an interlude. I haven't finished with you by a long shot."

"Oh?" She opened her blue eyes very wide and looked limpidly back at him. "You sound very sure of yourself."

He leaned closer. "Shouldn't I be?" There was a hint of laughter in his voice, and more than a hint of confidence. He looked like a man who knew what he wanted and knew also that what he wanted he would get.

It was unnerving, the reaction that look and voice produced in her. She waited a minute before she replied, very softly, "Go call for the pizza."

They left for the cape the following day and stayed for a week. It was a blissfully happy honeymoon followed by a equally happy summer spent in their small apartment, painting the walls and making the rounds of tag sales to find furniture. They were deeply in love and deeply happy.

It was a happiness that lasted exactly seven months. They both worked hard and they had practically no money, but they had each other. "I'm going to write my doctoral dissertation on 'One Thousand and One Ways to Cook Hamburger Meat,'" she would say as she dished up another plate of their staple food.

"What's wrong with hamburger?" he would demand. "It's nutritious, it's tasty, and it's cheap. The perfect food. You're a genius to have discovered it." And they would laugh and eat their dinner and fall into bed.

The idyll ended on January 6 when she went to the doctor and found out she was pregnant.

Chapter Three

࿔

"But I *can't* be pregnant," she had protested to the doctor, a gynecologist who was a friend of her father's. "I'm on the pill." On some issues, Mary was *not* more Catholic than the pope and this was one of them. Both she and Kit had agreed that children were something to be put off for the future.

The pill was not infallible, Dr. Murak told her gently, and she was most definitely pregnant. About three months along, actually. He told her not to worry, that he would be glad to take care of her. She was Bob's girl, after all, and there would be no charge. He had known her family for years and did not make the mistake of mentioning an abortion.

Kit was not so perceptive. After five minutes of incredulity, anger, and general agitation, he suggested that she get an abortion. Nothing in her entire life had ever shocked her more.

"But, Christ, Mary, we can't *afford* a baby," he stormed angrily. "I don't have a dime to my name. I work crazy hours—and so do you. What's going to happen to your fellowship if you have a baby? You'll have to give it up."

"Then I'll give it up," she had replied grimly.

"I don't want you to give it up!" he shouted. "I didn't marry you to make you give things up!"

"Would you rather make me a murderer?" she shouted back.

He thrust his hand through his thick hair, causing it to fall untidily over his forehead. "It isn't murder," he answered in a more controlled voice. "It's a perfectly legal operation."

"Oh God," she said, pressing shaking hands to her mouth and staring at him with horrified eyes. "How can you say this to me? You're talking about *our baby*." And she began to cry, harsh wracking sobs that hurt her throat and chest. After a minute he put his arms around her.

"It isn't that it's not important to me," he said, a note of quiet desperation in his voice. "It's that it's too important. A child needs security and he can't have security if there's no financial stability."

She was stiff within the circle of his arm, refusing the comfort of physical contact that he was offering. "Money isn't that important." She sobbed. "It's love that matters."

"You can say that," he answered grimly, "because you've never known what it's like to need money and not to have it." She was trying desperately to control her sobs and her body shook with the effort of containment. He held her for a minute and then said wearily, "All right, sweetheart, please don't upset yourself like this. We'll have the baby. I don't know how the hell I'm going to manage it, but I will. Somehow, I will."

They had patched the quarrel up, but a bitter seed had been sown. And then in March he got an offer to test for a role in a new film being shot by one of Hollywood's leading producers.

"He was in New Haven three weeks ago and saw me in the Tennessee Williams revival we're doing. He's making the movie version of *The Russian Experiment* and he wants me to test for the role of Ivan."

"Oh, Kit, how marvelous!" *The Russian Experiment* had been the blockbuster novel of the previous year, and they had both read it. It was a sophisticated combination of suspense, intrigue, and political and metaphysical speculation. Ivan was a young anarchist whose brooding and bitter presence had been a thread woven throughout the entire fabric of the novel. It would be a fabulous part if Kit could get it.

He had gotten it. The producer had liked his test and, with much hullabaloo about "discovering a new Brando," had signed him to a contract.

He had gone to California to make the movie and she stayed in Connecticut. He didn't want to take her away from her fellowship and then there was the baby. They both agreed it would be far more sensible for her to wait until the summer, until after the movie, after the baby, after the papers and finals, and then they would decide what they would do and where they would live. They closed up their apartment, stored their furniture in her mother's attic, and she went back home to live.

The female star of *The Russian Experiment* was

Jessica Corbet, an actress of international repute. She was beautiful and talented, and at thirty-two had gone through two husbands and several highly publicized affairs. According to the papers, she began a new one with Kit.

At first Mary didn't believe it. She was sophisticated enough to know that ninety percent of the gossip blazoned across the headlines of movie scandal sheets was untrue. If Kit had been more faithful about calling her, if he had written with any regularity, perhaps she would not have begun to doubt.

It was a terrible experience for her. She had been brought up in a close-knit, loving, and supportive family, and all her relationships had hitherto been deeply secure and unquestioned. When once the first trickle of doubt about Kit had been let in, it seemed as if the entire foundation of her marriage began to crumble. He hadn't really wanted to marry her, she thought. She had forced him into it by refusing to sleep with him. He didn't really want a wife. And he certainly didn't want a baby. He had made that very clear.

There was never any mention in the scandal sheets or the gossip columns that she read so feverishly of the fact that Christopher Douglas had a wife. It didn't occur to her that he might be trying to protect her. It did occur to her that he didn't want her anymore, was embarrassed to admit that America's hottest new sex symbol had a pregnant wife at home.

Whenever he called, which was not very frequently, he sounded distracted and very very distant. She couldn't ask him about any of the things she was reading in the paper. She could only be polite and cool and distant herself.

She finished her term at school and got, as usual, high honors. At the end of June, three weeks early, she went into labor. Her mother and father took her to the hospital and then tried to get hold of Kit. He wasn't at his apartment. He wasn't at the studio. Finally Mrs. O'Connor got his agent on the phone. Kit had gone off to Jessica Corbet's ranch for the weekend, he told Mary's distressed mother. He would see if he could contact him.

After 8 hours of labor, Mary's baby was born dead. The cord had caught around his neck during the delivery and he had strangled. Dr. Murak was devastated. "There was nothing I could do," he kept saying to Dr. O'Connor. "Nothing, Bob. It was just one of those freak things."

Mrs. O'Connor finally got hold of Kit at his apartment a day later. He flew into New Haven on the first flight, but when Mary opened her eyes to see him standing at her bedside, she had said only, "Go away. I never want to see you again." And she hadn't, until *Personality* had discovered her existence and precipitated his arrival on her doorstep.

The rain had stopped and she looked up at the gray Nantucket sky and saw a patch of blue over the water. The storm was passing over. She lifted her head, her wet black hair slicked back, and stood for a long time, staring at that blue sky. The storm always passes, she thought, if one only has the fortitude to wait it out.

It had been a year before her storm of grief and

guilt over the loss of her baby and the failure of her marriage had begun to abate. It had been a terrible year and sometimes she thought the only thing that had saved her sanity was her work. She threw herself into her studies with a feverish and grim intensity. By day, working in the library or attending classroom lectures and seminars, she kept the agony at bay.

It was at night that it overwhelmed her, and she would cry silently in her solitary bed. She blamed Kit. He became her scapegoat; on him she hung all the responsibility for their failure. *He* had run out on her when she needed him. *He* had not wanted the baby. It was desperately important that her consciousness should have someone else to take responsibility, because deep in her subconscious, she blamed herself. Although she tried, she could never forget that her first reaction to news of the baby had been dismay. That had changed, and as he had grown inside her her feelings had become warm and protective. But initially, she had not wanted him. Deep, deep inside her, her Irish Catholic upbringing was saying that God had punished her for that initial rejection. And the more she felt this the more feverishly she tried to blame Kit. Lying awake night after endless night, she began to understand what Thoreau had meant when he said "The mass of men live lives of quiet desperation."

She had thrown herself into her work and her work had saved her. None of her professors or her fellow students had ever mentioned Kit to her again. They behaved to her with the scrupulous and impersonal respect that her scholarly achievement commanded in their world. It was a world she clung to: a quiet and traditional place where only intellectual things counted.

In two years time she had her Ph.D., and the following January the university published her doctoral dissertation as a book. It established her scholarly reputation immediately. She was offered a job at a prestigious Massachusetts university and knew, if she produced as she was fully capable of doing, she would be given tenure. She had achieved a place for herself, a place worthy of reverence, and she had thought her life was settled.

And then Kit had come back.

Nothing had really changed, she told herself as she walked back to her brother's cottage through the brightening day. She still had her job. The university had stood behind her: her colleagues had been supportive and unquestioning, her students had been fiercely protective, the university security force had acted as her bodyguards. It would all die down and by September be forgotten.

Only she would not forget. She had seen his movies; why, then, she thought despairingly, should seeing him again in person have had such an effect on her? When she at last reached the cottage, her face was once again wet, but not this time from the rain.

She left Nantucket the following day and went back to her own house to do laundry and repack for her three-week sojourn in New Hampshire. She arrived home on Saturday night and was to leave again Monday morning. Sunday afternoon, taking a break from the ironing board, she called her parents. Her father answered the phone.

"Hi, Daddy," she said cheerfully. "It's me. How are you doing?"

"We're just fine, honey," he answered. "How are you?" There was a cautious note to his inquiry that puzzled her.

"Great," she replied. "The weather on Nantucket was super and Mike and Kathy and the kids were just what I needed. So sane, if you know what I mean."

He chuckled. "I don't know if I'd call my grandchildren sane, precisely, but I know what you mean."

"I feel like a bird on the wing. I had wanted to get down to see you and Mother but I leave for Yarborough bright and early tomorrow morning. I won't see you until August, I guess."

"You're still going to Yarborough?"

"Of course I'm still going to Yarborough. Daddy, what's wrong? You sound funny. Is mother all right?"

"Your mother's fine," he assured her. "She'll be sorry she missed your call. She's out playing tennis with Sue Bayley. The town tournament starts next week and they've entered the doubles competition."

"Oh. Well, wish her luck for me and give her my love. I'll send you a postcard from Yarborough."

"Yes, you do that." Her father's voice came strongly now over the wire. "Have a good time, honey. And—give the place a chance, will you? Remember, things aren't always what they seem to be."

"You sound like Hamlet," she replied in a puzzled voice. "Are you sure everything's okay at home, Daddy?"

"Positive."

"All right, then, Daddy, I'll say good-bye for now."

"Good-bye, Mary Kate. Call us if you need us."

"I will. Good-bye." She hung up the phone and stood staring at it doubtfully for a full minute. What on earth had gotten into her father?

Chapter Four

Yarborough College was set on a crystal-clear lake in the foothills of the White Mountains. It had been founded eighty years ago as a small men's liberal-arts college and had managed to survive with much of its original character intact. It offered its students—who now included women—an excellent academic program coupled with one of the best ski schools in the country. In the summer it ran its now-famous drama school and festival. Of the last five productions to come out of the festival, three had gone on to Broadway.

Mary had never been to Yarborough herself but she had seen pictures of the campus and she was looking forward to the idyllic peace and serenity promised by such a lovely setting. Her own schedule called for her to deliver one hour-and-a-half lecture a day. Her students, who were all also involved in the production of the play that opened at the beginning of August, would receive six graduate credits for the summer school. The stipend she was to receive for giving the lectures was nominal, but room and board was included, and her lectures covered material she knew thoroughly and so had not taken a tremendous amount of work for her to put together. All in all, she was looking forward to relaxing in the beautiful New Hampshire summer.

As she turned in to the gates of the campus she was surprised to see a crowd of people standing on the drive. She braked the car and someone shouted, "It's her!" Cameras started to flash and questions were shouted. Very frightened, Mary gripped the wheel of the car and a man in a guard uniform opened her door and said, "Move over, Dr. O'Connor, I'll drive you in."

Obediently she slid over and in a minute the man had the car moving briskly forward. The reporters all jumped aside, and as the car moved up the drive another guard firmly slammed the huge iron gate shut.

"My God," said Mary faintly. "What was that all about?"

The guard smiled briefly. "You're Mrs. Christopher Douglas, aren't you?"

"Are they *still* harping on that?" she said incredulously.

"They've been here for almost a week now, I'm afraid. Nasty lot." The car came to a halt in front of a venerable old brick building and a slim, wiry man came running down the steps. "Here's Mr. Clark," said her escort.

"Dr. O'Connor?" The director of the festival opened the door of the Buick and Mary got out and offered her hand.

"Yes. Hello, Mr. Clark. What a fuss at the gate!"

"Isn't it terrible?" he replied, looking not at all distressed. "I've put you in one of the summer cottages we had built a few years ago especially for the festival. I'll drive with you over there and we can unload your luggage. Then, if you like, I'll give you a quick tour of the campus."

"That sounds great," Mary agreed. The guard got out of the car and she and George Clark got in.

"Turn left at the bottom of the drive here," he said and she accelerated slowly.

The cottage she had been alotted was charming: small and rustic, with a bedroom, a sitting room, and a screened-in porch. "Meals are served in the dining room," Mr. Clark told her. "I'm afraid we all eat together: professionals and students alike. It's supposed to be part of the charm of the program."

She smiled reassuringly. "I'm sure it is, Mr. Clark."

"George, please," he answered. "We're very informal here in the summer."

"Then you must call me Mary." She looked around her. The row of cottages was set in the side of hill and surrounded by huge pines. The sparkle of the lake was just visible through the trees. "It's like a summer resort," she said, half humorously.

"I hope you are going to enjoy yourself," he replied with a warm smile. "We didn't ask you here just to work."

They walked around the campus and Mary found herself liking George Clark very much. He was not precisely good-looking but his narrow face and quick, nervous hands, were oddly attractive. They talked about her lectures and she told him a little of what she had planned. He was pleased and encouraging and told her something about the students she would be working with.

"How is the play shaping up?" she asked curiously. "You've been rehearsing for a week now, haven't you?"

"Yes. And the most damnable thing has just happened. We've lost our Gertrude."

"Oh no," she said with sympathetic concern. Gertrude was Hamlet's mother in the play and it was a central role. "You had Maud Armitage, didn't you? What happened?"

"She broke her ankle on the tennis court."

"Good heavens."

"That is putting it mildly. I have a New York agent scouring the earth for a replacement—hopefully an actress who has done the part before. Time is getting short. It's only three weeks until we open. That's the one great drawback of this summer school—there just isn't enough time."

"Well, it's Hamlet who is really important," she said soothingly. "How is Adrian Saunders managing?" They were walking up the path leading to the building that housed the English and drama departments, and at these words of hers he stopped dead. "Is something the matter?" she asked.

"Is it possible you don't know . . .?" He was staring at her in stunned surprise.

"Know what?" Her voice was sharp with alarm.

"Adrian Saunders backed out at the last minute," he said slowly. "He got a movie offer and of course he wanted to take it. So we got someone else to play Hamlet."

She felt a warning prickle of apprehension. "Who?" she asked tensely and was not surprised when the answer came.

"Christopher Douglas."

Her first impulse was to run. She went back to her cottage and set for a long time on the front porch, her hands clasped into tense fists, staring out at the pines. Two things finally got her on her feet and into the bedroom to unpack. One was the knowledge that if she backed out now, George Clark would be left without a teacher for his course. The other was her father's advice about giving Yarborough a chance. Obviously he had known Kit was going to be here. And he had not told her, had let her come in ignorance of what she would find. Her father, she remembered, had always liked Kit.

So she unpacked, showered and changed into a blue shirt-dress, and made her way slowly over to the dining hall. Sherry, George had told her, was served before dinner in the recreation room of the dining hall. She opened the door of the spacious, high-ceilinged room, stepped over the threshhold and saw him immediately. He was surrounded by a pack of girls and seemed to be listening patiently to what one of them was saying. It was such a familiar pose to her: the turn of his head as it bent a little toward the favored person, the clear-cut profile. . . . He looked up and saw her. He dropped his fan club instantly and came across the room, moving like a panther with long, graceful, silent strides.

He stopped in front of her and she said, "I didn't know you were here."

"Yes," he replied. "So George told me." His eyes on

her face were as black as coal. "Would you have come if you'd known?"

"No." She stared at him and her lovely full mouth tightened with temper. "*Why*, Kit? You knew I was lecturing here. There was a crowd of reporters at the gate when I came in. It's going to be horrible."

"I thought it was time I tried something more serious," he replied. "And I wanted to get back to the stage. When my agent called and told me the Yarborough Festival needed a Hamlet quickly, I took it. I knew you'd be here, of course, but as the truth of our relationship has already leaked, I didn't see what harm could be done by my coming too."

She glared at him, her back rigid. "There's no harm to you, of course, you're probably used to people shouting at you and snapping your picture every time you go around the corner. I, thank God, am not accustomed to being perpetually hounded in such a fashion. And I don't *want* to get accustomed to it. I am absolutely furious with you for doing this to me."

Her eyes shot blue fire at him. Infuriatingly, he grinned. "Now, now, don't get your Irish up, Princess." A man appeared at her elbow and he said, "I don't think you know Mel Horner, my agent. This is Dr. O'Connor, Mel, of whom you have heard much."

Princess. He used to call her Princess when . . . "How do you do, Mr. Horner," she got out and offered her hand. Somewhere a bell rang and they were all moving into dinner. She found herself between George Clark and Frank Moore, a nice boy from Kit's old drama school who was to play Laertes. Kit was sitting opposite her, flanked by the pretty student who was to play Ophelia and a young art student who was working on the set. She was also very pretty.

Everyone but Mary had been in residence for a week and they all seemed to be quite comfortable with each other. The girls were obviously overwhelmed by Kit and hung on his every word with breathless attention. Mary sat quietly and let the conversation flow around her.

"What did you think of the costume sketches, Chris?" George asked.

"I liked them." Kit took a sip out of his glass. He was drinking milk. "I think not quite so much velvet, though? We may be in New England but it is summer after all."

"True," George agreed. "And the lights can get pretty hot."

A little silence fell as Kit attacked his pot roast. He had always been a good trencherman, Mary remembered. He ate little breakfast and lunch, but he liked his dinner.

"I've wanted to ask you something about your last picture, Chris," said Carolyn Nash, the pretty Ophelia. "Did you *really* do your own stunt work?" She had large, pansy-brown eyes and they were directed worshipfully up at his dark face.

"Yes." He smiled a little ruefully. "I must say I kept on suggesting they get a professional stunt guy in, but the director never saw it that way. Unfortunately."

"Why not?" asked Mary suddenly. There had been some very dangerous scenes in his last film, she recalled.

"Saving money, I expect," he replied and ate another forkful of meat.

Mel Horner snorted. "Don't you believe it. They didn't get a stunt man because no one else looks like Chris. More important—no one moves like he does. But he was quite safe, Dr. O'Connor, I assure you."

Mary was intensely annoyed. "I'm quite sure that Kit can take care of himself," she said sweetly.

At her use of that name the two girls' heads swung around and they stared at her, big-eyed and speculative. "Kit?" said Carolyn on a note of inquiry.

Mary stared at him in exasperation. "It's a nickname for Christopher," he said blandly and smiled kindly into Carolyn's small face.

She looked like a kitten that has just been stroked. "Why do you say Chris was safe doing those stunts?" she asked Mel innocently.

"He's much too valuable a property for a production company to allow anything to happen to him," Mel said bluntly. "There aren't many stars around these days whose very name guarantees a stampede at the box office."

Kit shot a look at his agent and Mary said even more sweetly than before, "I suppose that's true."

Black eyes stared at her face for a minute and then he asked, with precisely the same intonation she had used, "And did you graduate summa cum laude *again*?"

She looked thoughtfully back and then, suddenly, smiled. "I'm sorry."

He made a brief gesture with his hand. "Okay." And he went back to eating his dinner.

"I don't know how you stay so thin and eat so much," complained Mel, looking with envy at his client. Mel had a very pronounced potbelly.

"He basically only eats one meal a day," Mary replied absently. She realized what she had said and flushed. "At least he did."

"I still do." There was definite amusement in Kit's deep beautiful voice.

"I have a friend in one of your courses, Dr. O'Connor," Frank Moore said to her and she turned to him in relief.

"Oh? Who is that?"

"Jim Henley."

"Oh, yes." Mary smiled. "I know Mr. Henley. He's in my senior seminar."

"I have to confess I wrote and asked him what you were like when we knew you would be giving the lectures this summer."

"Oh?" She sipped her water.

"And what did this Jim Henley say?" asked Kit mischievously.

"He sent me back a telegram." Frank grinned. "It had only two words on it: Drool Drool."

Kit laughed and so did Mel Horner and George Clark. Mary, who had developed a technique for dealing with drooling male students, said coolly, "Did he? How disappointing. I thought Mr. Henley had the makings of a scholar."

Frank Moore flushed and George Clark and Mel Horner sobered immediately. Only Kit still had a wicked glint in his eyes.

"That's the girl," he said encouragingly. "I bet that cool expression really keeps them at a distance."

She bit her lip. The trouble with Kit, she thought, was he always could make her laugh. She wrinkled her nose at him. "It does."

His eyes laughed back at her but after a minute he turned to Mel Horner. "By the way, Mel, I want you to arrange a press conference. Tomorrow afternoon will be as good a time as any I suppose."

Mel Horner's mouth dropped open. "A press conference?" he almost squeaked. "You never hold press conferences. I've been begging you for years . . ."

"Well, I will hold one tomorrow," said Kit with ominous calm. "What's more, I think the rest of the cast should be there. And George as well."

"Are you serious, Chris?"

"I am perfectly serious. It's the only way to put all these unfortunate rumors to rest. I do not," he said with devastating simplicity, "want the press to disturb my wife."

Chapter Five

❧

Tuesday morning Mary delivered her first lecture. There were thirty-five students in the festival program, some of them members of the cast and the rest involved in other aspects of the production. She knew that the young eyes watching her so assessingly were more interested in her relationship to their leading man than they were in her academic record. Well, she thought grimly, they were damn well going to be in for a shock.

The first thing she did was to hand out a reading list. Eyes popped open and a male voice asked incredulously, "Do you really expect us to read all these books?"

The speaker was the tall, broad-shouldered, blond boy who was playing Fortinbras. Physically a good foil for Kit, she thought, before she answered, "Certainly I do. You are all receiving six graduate credits for this summer school. I rather imagined you would expect to work for them."

"Well, we *are* working," replied the boy. He gave her a lazy, charming grin. "I don't at all object to sitting in class with you, Dr. O'Connor. In fact, it's a pleasure. But between rehearsals and daily lectures, I really don't see how we can possibly get all this reading done."

Mary looked severely into the handsome, boyish face. "That, Mr. Lindquist, sounds to me both unscholarly and insincere. Are you *quite* sure you wish to remain enrolled in this summer school?"

There was absolute silence in the classroom. Then Eric Lindquist said quietly, "Yes, I'm sure. I apologize, Dr. O'Connor."

"Your apology is accepted." She glanced around the class. "Are there any further questions? No? Good. My topic for today is the place of drama in Renaissance England." The students obediently picked up their pens.

The press conference was held that afternoon in the recreation room of the dining hall. Mel Horner, taking full advantage of his client's unusual mood, had made a few telephone calls, and as a result there were representatives from the New York press and the wire services as well as the usual fan and scandal sheets. George Clark served as a general host, and while they were waiting for Kit to arrive, he and the other cast members circulated among the press, answering questions about the production and even more questions about Mr. and Mrs. Douglas.

"I don't know much about her at all," Frank Moore said cheerfully to an inquisitive reporter. "She's supposed to be a terrific Renaissance scholar. I haven't read her book yet, but it made quite a stir in the academic world. If today's lecture is anything to go on, the reputation is deserved. She knows her stuff. What's more—she makes it interesting."

George Clark, the only one besides Kit and Mel Horner who knew the real circumstances behind Kit's presence at his festival, lied gamely. "No, it was a complete accident. Neither of them realized the other was coming to Yarborough."

"How do they act toward each other, Mr. Clark?" shot an eager woman reporter.

"As two civilized people," snapped George in return. He was beginning to realize why Kit did not give press conferences. He noticed a small movement at the door and then Kit came quietly in. He was dressed casually in a navy golf shirt and tan pants and he stood in the doorway, making no sound and slowly looking around the room. Gradually, without his seeming to do anything at all to attract it, the attention of the room swung his way and the place erupted into chaos. George Clark suddenly found himself a little shaken at the thought of directing Christopher Douglas. Magnetism like that was something that came along perhaps once in a generation.

Mel Horner stepped to the mike that had been set up and spoke into it. "Now, ladies and gentlemen. Mr. Douglas will be happy to answer your questions, but they really must come one at a time." He looked nervously at Kit and thought, I hope the hell he keeps his temper.

He did. He put on what Mel afterward told him

was perhaps the finest performance of his career. He disdained the microphone and pitched his celebrated voice to an easily audible level. "I thought perhaps that first I would explain a little about my marital situation since it seems to have provoked such universal interest." He didn't sound at all sarcastic and he smiled charmingly before he went on to give a very edited account of his marriage: "We were both students and too young. It simply didn't work out." The coincidence of himself and Dr. O'Connor—he scrupulously called her Dr. O'Connor the whole time—both working at the Yarborough Festival this summer was just that, a coincidence. He had not realized until after he took the role that she would be lecturing here. "So you see," he concluded disarmingly, "it has all been a tempest in a teapot."

"But why didn't you ever get a divorce, Chris?" asked the man from *Personality*.

"Neither of us ever got around to it, that's all. If I had wanted to marry again, I would have. I'm sure we'll do something permanent eventually. We've just both been rather busy these last years."

"Why did you keep your marriage such a secret?" It was the eager young lady from one of the wire services.

He shrugged. "It was over with before I became established. The subject never came up. And I certainly didn't want Dr. O'Connor bothered by a lot of unnecessary questions." He gestured beautifully around the room. "As has happened."

"Is that why you're holding this press conference? To protect—ah, Dr. O'Connor?" It was a man from a New Hampshire paper.

Kit looked at him thoughtfully. "Partly. I feel guilty about having caused her all this trouble. But I was hoping, too, that there might be some interest in my tackling such a formidable role. After all, I haven't done any theater in five years and my movie roles have hardly been of this caliber."

"How do you feel about Hamlet?" asked the man from the Associated Press and from then on the conference moved into theatrical areas. Kit wandered around the room, chatting pleasantly, patiently answering questions, utterly relaxed, utterly charming.

"I don't believe what I'm seeing," muttered Mel Horner to George Clark. "*Chris* of all people. He hates things like this."

"John Andrews was right, of course," replied George soberly. "He's doing it to protect Mary."

Mel looked at him accusingly. "You haven't told anyone that Chris asked to come here?"

"Of course not!"

"Good. The fat would really be in the fire if the press found that out."

"Or if Mary did."

"True." Mel Horner sighed. "What a shame to waste a woman like that in the classroom. That skin! Those eyes! She could make a fortune in the movies."

George grinned. "Somehow, gorgeous as she undoubtedly is, I cannot see Mary in the movies."

Mel Horner thought for a minute. "I suppose you're right," he replied gloomily. "The problem is I can't see her as Chris's wife either, and I'm afraid that that is what he wants."

They both looked at the slim, dark man who was

sitting casually now on the arm of a chair talking to a New York theater critic. "He seems a very decent sort," said George Clark, "but it's a hell of a life, isn't it?"

Mary stayed as far as possible from the press conference. Her brief experience with the media after the bombshell of her marriage had dropped had been enough to permanently scar her sensibilities. What a life Kit must lead, she thought, with a flicker of genuine horror. Still, he had known what it would be like and he had gone after it with a single-minded intensity, ruthlessly sacrificing everything else to this one driving ambition. Having been one of the things sacrificed, she hoped that at least to him the result was worth the price.

She spent the early part of the afternoon in the library and then, when she thought the press must be gone, she changed her clothes and went down to the lake. The college had almost half a mile of lakefront property, with a dock, an area of lawn chairs, and a volleyball court. Mary sat down in one of the chairs and stared out at the sparkling water.

"The press conference went very well," said a rumbling voice in her ear, and she turned to see Alfred Block, the actor who was playing Claudius, Hamlet's uncle. Block was a well-known actor from the Broadway stage who had never managed to break into movies. He was in his middle forties, with dark brown hair that was beginning to thin. His eyes were gray with the hint of a slant that was oddly surprising in his otherwise Anglo-Saxon face.

"It's over then," she replied with a restrained smile. "I thought it would be safe for me to emerge from my hiding place."

"Where do you hide, Mary, when you want to escape?"

"The library, where else?" she replied lightly, not liking the way he was looking at her. There were two young students stretched out on the dock, both wearing bathing suits and showing a lot more flesh than she was in her khaki shorts and plaid shirt. Why didn't he go leer at them, she thought with exasperation. Alfred Block had cornered her over coffee in the recreation room last night and she had heard more about him and his career than she ever cared to know. She was afraid the man was going to make a dreadful pest of himself and was wondering how best to handle him when Kit arrived.

"Thank God that's over," he announced, as he flopped down on the grass at her feet and closed his eyes.

"Don't let us disturb your rest," said Mary testily.

"I won't," he mumbled, his eyes still closed. She stared at him for a minute as he lay there on the grass with his feet crossed, his hands clasped behind his head, his eyes closed against the sun. She was suddenly intensely aware of him, of the rise and fall of his chest with his even breathing, of the beat of the pulse at the base of his tanned throat, of the latent power in the length of his lean body. . . . She took a deep breath and reached out to kick him in the ribs with her sneaker-shod foot.

"Hey!" he yelled indignantly, and sat up.

"I want to hear what happened at the press conference," she said sweetly.

"That hurt." He rubbed his side and glared at her reproachfully.

"You're tough," she answered even more sweetly. "You run along the tops of moving trains, you hang from cliffs, you punch out thugs, how can a little nudge in the side hurt you?"

"That was more than a nudge." He looked at her speculatively. "You've seen my movies." His voice was soft, dangerously soft, and the glint in his dark eyes was more dangerous still.

Mary was absolutely furious with herself. "Yes," she snapped. "I've seen your movies."

"I should imagine," put in the insinuating voice of Alfred Block, "that all the world has seen your movies, Chris. Especially that last little adventure film. *How* much money has it grossed?"

The two girls who were sunning themselves on the dock had been slowly moving their way ever since Kit had arrived. Hearing Alfred's question, one of them eagerly volunteered an answer. "I read in *Variety* that it may eventually be the biggest-grossing movie ever."

"Really?" Mary looked at the girl, glad of any excuse that would direct her attention away from Kit. "Has it done that well?"

"Oh, yes." The young face glowed at Kit. She was a very pretty girl, golden brown from the sun, with long, sun-bleached hair and widely spaced green eyes.

He looked back at her with pleasure, his eyes going over the smooth expanse of tanned young skin. He turned back to Mary. "You're going to be red as a lobster if you stay out too long in this sun."

Devil, thought Mary, amused in spite of herself. She met his eyes and made a face. "I'm afraid you're right." She held out an arm and regarded it appraisingly. "It's just turning nicely pink." She leaned back in her chair. "However, before I go, what happened at the press conference?"

"I think I put to rest all their speculation about you and me, if that's what you mean."

"Yes, that's what I mean. Will they—go away now?"

He shrugged. "Most of them." He looked up suddenly and his eyes locked with hers. It was almost as if he had touched her. "You'll be safe," he said deeply.

She pushed herself to her feet. "Good," she replied through a suddenly dry throat and knew, as she walked up the stairs from the lakefront lawn, that so long as he was around she wasn't safe at all. She would simply have to keep out of his way, which considering the small size of the school and the fact that they took all their meals together, was not going to be easy. What she needed, she thought, was someone to act as a buffer between her and Kit. She thought about the various possibilities as she slowly climbed the hill that led to her cottage in the pines. Not Alfred Block—he was too nasty; not Frank Moore—he was too vulnerable; not Eric Lindquist—he was too cocky. George. The name flashed into her brain and she smiled with satisfaction. Of course. He was very nice, intelligent, talented—and old and sophisticated enough not to think she meant more than she really did.

She arrived at her cottage and went in to shower

and change for dinner in a suddenly confident frame
of mind. Kit thought he was so damn irresistible—
well she would show him. The stinker, she thought, as
she blew her hair dry. I'll fix him for coming here and
putting me in this horrible position.

Chapter Six

❧

Mary put her plan into action at dinner. She made sure she entered the dining room with George, and it seemed very natural when she took a seat beside him at the table. During dinner she devoted almost her entire attention to his conversation, and under the heady spell of her blue eyes, he seemed to grow at least two inches.

Mary never flirted. Whenever she wanted to charm a man she simply sat quietly, looked beautiful, and listened. It was a devastating technique and had soothed the wounded breasts of many affronted male professors who had originally objected to the appointment of so young a woman to the faculty of their illustrious university.

Back in the recreation room she sat on a sofa, allowed George to bring her coffee, and for the first time that evening looked directly at Kit. He was standing against the great brick fireplace, holding a cup of coffee and he was, as always, surrounded by a crowd of girls. Across the shining blond and brown heads their eyes met. Mary, not a bad actress herself, produced a cool indifferent smile, leaned back and crossed her long and elegant legs. George returned with her coffee and she greeted him with a noticeably warmer smile.

Carolyn Nash, following the direction of Kit's eyes, said, "Dr. O'Connor sure surprised us this morning. She gave out a reading list as long as my arm. The worst part of it is, she seems to expect us to actually *do* the reading."

Kit's eyes came back to her pretty face. "Of course she does. Dr. O'Connor takes her job seriously."

"Well, so do I. But my job is to play Ophelia."

"You have Ophelia's lines down letter perfect," he said, "so you don't need to spend time on them. Have you always been such a quick study?"

She blossomed under his attention and was about to answer when another girl, the sun-bleached girl from the lake, broke in. "You're the one with the long part, Chris! The longest part Shakespeare ever wrote. I think it's marvelous that you have so much of it down already."

He replied absently and continued to stand there, islanded by adoring girls, his real attention somewhere else. Mary's shoulder-length hair had drifted like black silk across the cushion she was leaning against; her relaxed, slender body in its green summer dress was half sitting, half reclining on the soft, cushiony sofa. She tipped back her head and laughed at something George Clark said to her. As Kit watched, Alfred Block drew up a chair next to Mary's sofa and broke into the conversation. After five minutes the group was joined by Frank Moore.

Mary yawned daintily, put down her empty cup and rose. She shared a general smile among her admirers, made a remark Kit couldn't hear, and moved to the door. Three men hurried to open it for her. She left, alone. Kit dropped his retinue and went after her.

She was going up the path through the pines that led to her cottage when he caught up with her. He didn't say anything, just fell into step next to her and continued the uphill climb. Finally she could stand the silence no longer and said, "I don't believe your way lies in this direction."

At that he reached out and grasped her arm, forcing her to stop. They had come out of the woods by now and were on the paved road that ran along the front of the five summer cottages alotted to various members of the festival staff. The road was lit by a single light posted high on a wooden pole and he stopped her under its pale illumination. With hard fingers around her wrist he held her left hand up to the light. "You're still wearing my ring," he said. "You're still my wife, and by God you're going to act like it. Leave poor George alone. You'll knock him right off his feet and you don't want him. You're only using him to teach me a lesson."

He was perfectly right of course and his perceptiveness made her furious. She jerked her hand away from his. "Leave me alone," she said in a trembling voice. "I was doing just fine until you came bulldozing your way back into my life. You knew I was going to be here when you came. If you don't like what you see, then you'll just have to lump it."

She turned to leave him and he reached out and caught her once again, this time by the waist. She twisted against his grip, struggling to get away from him, and he pinned her arms behind her, holding her so that she faced him. Mary felt the brief impact of his body against hers and she stiffened. She stared up into his dark dark eyes. "What do you want, Kit?" Her voice sounded breathless and she hoped he would put it down to the struggle.

His eyes, darkly lashed and unfathomable, looked back at her. "You," he said. "I want you." They stayed like that for a long minute, their eyes locked, their bodies scarcely an inch apart. His eyes were unfathomable no longer; no woman with a single normal instinct could fail to recognize what was glimmering there now. Her eyes fell before that look.

"I thought that was it," she said in a low voice. "When George told me you were here, I knew you had come to persecute me."

"I don't want to persecute you, Princess." His voice was deeper than usual, dark and husky. He released her wrists and slid his hands up her bare arms to her shoulders. "I want you to come back to me. Be my wife again. I do want you most damnably." And he bent his head and kissed her.

It was like coming home again. It was that feeling that frightened her most, frightened her more than the flooding sweetness of her unplanned response. The feel of his arms around her, his body hard against hers, his mouth on her mouth . . . When she was with him like this it was the only time she stopped thinking and just felt.

But he hadn't brought her quite that far yet. Some

remnants of sanity still remained, enough at any rate to enable her to pull free of his embrace. "No," she said, unsteadily but definitely. "No. We tried it once and it didn't work. I'm not going to put myself through that hell again."

He pushed his black hair back off his forehead. "You never gave me a chance. I was *not* having an affair with Jessica Corbet. That was all media hype."

She stared at him incredulously. "Are you serious? The yacht—the trip to Rome—you were alone with her all that time and you never made love to her? You can't possibly expect me to believe that."

"That was *after*," he replied stubbornly. "After you told me you never wanted to see me again, after I wrote you two letters and never got an answer. Then I thought, hell, I might as well be hung for a sheep as a lamb. But while we were really married, I was faithful to you."

"Faithful?" There was unmistakable bitterness in her voice. "Do you call it faithful to call once every two weeks and talk for three minutes? Do you call it faithful to never even *attempt* to explain what was behind all the headlines. What the hell did you expect me to think?"

"I expected you to trust me. You never asked me about Jessica at all."

"No." She stepped away from him a little farther. "No. And I'm not asking now. Your private life has nothing to do with me any longer."

"It's that goddamn pride of yours," he said savagely.

"Pride is about all you've left me, Kit!" she flashed back. "My pride and my job. It took me a long hard time to regain the one and to earn the other and I'm not risking either again."

"You kissed me back just now," he said. "You can't pretend you're indifferent to me, Mary."

"We always did strike sparks from each other. It's what got us married in the first place. But marriage is more than making love, Kit. You and I may be good at that part of it, but we were dismal failures at the rest."

"We're older now," he said persuasively.

"I know, which is why I have the sense this time to say no and mean it." His face looked as bleak as winter and she sighed. "It wasn't all your fault, Kit. You're right, I was too proud to ask you to explain, too proud to show you how hurt I was. Perhaps now I'd do things differently. But you can't turn the clock back, Kit. We had our chance and we blew it. The people we were then don't exist anymore."

"I don't believe that," he said. "Mary . . ." There was the sound of laughter down the path. "Hell!" he said explosively under his breath.

She looked up at him sadly. "There really isn't anything else to be said. And I would appreciate it if in future you had a thought for my reputation. What are people going to think when they meet you coming down the path from my cottage?"

"They won't think a thing," he replied and after a minute produced a faintly mocking grin. "I have the cottage next to yours."

She did not get much sleep that night. Somehow she had not expected him to be so direct in his approach; she had not expected him to want her back as his wife. She had thought that, as always, he simply wanted to sleep with her.

As she lay awake into the small hours of the morning, however, the realization came to her that that was what he did want, that that was what marriage meant to him. It was not what it meant to her, however. She had grown up a great deal in the past four years and she knew that they had failed previously because both of them had been too self-absorbed to reach out of their own needs and desires to consider the needs and desires of the other. Kit had been so intent on his career that everything else, including her, had gone down before that drive like grass under a roller. He was so—single-minded. He always had been.

She would have to be the one to give in. If a marriage is to be successful, she thought, at least one partner must put it first. All those theories about men and women in equal partnership sounded lovely, but she had never seen it work successfully. One career had to give, one personality to yield. Particularly if there were children. You couldn't have your cake and eat it too, she thought bleakly.

What it all came down to was that what he offered her wasn't good enough. She loved him, she admitted that in the darkness and the privacy of her solitary bedroom; she would never feel for another man what she felt for him. She even understood why he was the way he was. He had always been on his own; his mother had died when he was very young and his father had remarried and then died a year later, leaving Kit in the care of an indifferent stepmother. He had grown up learning how to fend for himself and he had learned to be ruthless. Once he decided what he

wanted, he went after it; and if anything came between him and his desire, he walked over it without
rancor and without pity. It had been like that with the
baby. And then with her.

Now he had decided he wanted her again. He
wanted her to leave her home, her family and friends,
the peaceful fulfillment of her work—and for what?
To live a life she loathed and feared, where you
couldn't go out to dinner without being followed and
photographed, where every shiver in your relationship
was blazoned across the front pages of horrible news-
papers, where there was no peace and no silence. And
for what? For the nights that could make the universe
shudder? But what of the days? And the long, lonely
times when he was gone on location. And the other
women, beautiful and available, always so tantalizingly within his reach?

No. No. No. She would never go back to being
Mrs. Christopher Douglas.

Chapter Seven

❧

Mary finally fell asleep about four in the morning and three hours later her alarm rang. She felt heavy-eyed and sluggish as she made her way down the path to the dining room. She collected coffee and a muffin from the buffet and sat down at an empty table. There was no sign of Kit.

She finished her coffee and went to get a second cup. When she arrived back at her table it was to find she had company. Eric Lindquist was sitting there, and as she reseated herself he gave her his endearing boyish grin. The Sunshine Kid, Mary thought sourly, and started on her second cup of coffee.

"Have you heard who George snagged to play Gertrude?" he asked enthusiastically.

"No. Who?" She was not in a talkative mood.

"Margot Chandler." Mary's eyes widened and he laughed. "I'm not kidding, Dr. O'Connor. Margot Chandler has actually consented to play Hamlet's mother."

"She's too young," Mary said incredulously.

"Not really. She must be at least forty-five. Well preserved is the proper word for her, I think."

"Has she ever done any stage work?"

"Not to my knowledge." His grin widened. "This is definitely a 'Hollywood Goes Arty' summer at Yarborough."

"Kit has played Shakespeare on stage many times," Mary said astringently and suppressed a sudden urge to smack the handsome young face across from her. There was nothing on earth worse than a condescending twenty-two-year-old, she decided.

"Actually, I know he has. He had a damn good reputation at drama school—they still talk about him. But I'm certain as hell that Margot Chandler hasn't ever put her luscious mouth around a Shakespearean phrase."

"What on earth was George *thinking* of?" Mary asked despairingly.

"Well, he didn't have a whole lot of time to pick and choose. And apparently La Chandler has decided that her days of playing sexy leading ladies are numbered and so she had better look for a new metier for her talents. I shouldn't be at all surprised if Liz Taylor's big hit in *The Little Foxes* galvanized her. And, then, few women would pass up the chance of acting with Chris." His blue eyes were widely innocent in his suntanned face.

"As his *mother*?" Mary asked ironically. Eric grinned. He rather overdid that boyish smile, she thought cynically, and rose. "I'll see you in class," she said.

"Sure thing." He paused. "Mary," he added tentatively.

She stopped, turned and looked at him. She had always maintained a carefully formal relationship with all her students. It had been necessary. She was only a few years older than most of them and she was well aware of her own sexual attractiveness. But everyone at the summer school was on a first-name basis and she was here for too short a time for any of the boys to have a chance to become overly familiar. So she smiled briefly at Eric, nodded, and went on her way.

Her lecture on the Elizabethan concept of tragedy went very well. The students seemed resigned to the fact that she expected them to work and a few even became quite enthusiastic in a discussion she initiated on the concept of catharsis as it applied to Shakespearean tragedy. After the class was finished they all disappeared in the direction of the theater. Mary's lecture went from nine to ten-thirty and after that they rehearsed.

Mary took her books back to her cottage and decided to run into town to the drugstore. Accordingly, she got into her car and headed toward the college gates. There didn't appear to be any reporters around and she drove in a relaxed frame of mind. She did her shopping and was coming out of the store when the now-familiar flash went off. She stared for a moment in angry frustration at the man who was now approaching her. He had curly brown hair, a crooked nose, and was wearing a shirt that was halfway open, showing what Mary thought was a disgusting amount of hairy chest. She hated men who didn't button their shirts. He trained a smile at full tooth power straight at her. "Hi," he said ingratiatingly. "I'm Jason Razzia, free-lance writer and photographer. I'm planning an article on you and Chris, Mrs. Douglas. I wonder if I could talk to you for a few minutes."

"I have nothing to say to you, Mr. Razzia," she replied coldly. "And I do *not* wish to have my picture taken. I would appreciate your going away and leaving me alone."

"Aw, come on now, it's my livelihood, you know," he said coaxingly. "Just a few short questions. Like is it true that you and Chris are getting back together again?"

"No, it is *not* true," she said firmly. "I wish I could make you understand that there is no story here, Mr. Razzia. Mr. Douglas and I have ended our relationship and we have no intention of resurrecting it. That is all. Good-bye. And please go away." She walked to her car, got in and slammed the door. He took two more pictures of her before she drove away.

Mary was seething as she drove back to school. For the past month of her life she had felt positively hunted, and it was all Kit's fault. He could have played Hamlet out in California somewhere. Why did he have to come to Yarborough to do it?

She worked for an hour or so in the library after lunch, looking up some material for an article she was planning on Elizabethan songbooks. As always, the academic discipline soothed her nerves and she was in a calmer frame of mind when she walked down to the waterfront later in the afternoon. Rehearsal had ended and the lawn was filled with people, some swimming, some playing volleyball and others simply soaking up the sun. Mary had her bathing suit on under a terry-cloth sundress, and when she reached the waterfront she stood to unzip the cover-up while her eyes automatically searched the area for Kit. She didn't see him and so she dropped her dress on a chair with her sandals and towel and made for the lake.

There were a few students stretched out on the dock as she walked out to dive off and the male eyes all regarded her approvingly. She wore a plain navy maillot suit that showed off her slender figure tastefully but unmistakably. Her skin was like magnolia petals. She pulled her black hair back on the nape of her neck and secured it with an elastic band. Then she dove into the water.

It was cold. She came up gasping for breath, treaded water and looked around her. There were three rubber boats floating about in the water near her, two of them occupied by couples and one apparently empty. The lake was not very wide at this particular point and there was no sign of other boats. Mary struck out for the other side.

She was an excellent swimmer, not fast, but strong and steady. The youngsters on shore watched her unwavering progress toward the far side of the lake. And they watched as well the yellow rubber boat that followed her.

Mary didn't see the boat until she was three quarters of the way across. She paused then to tread water and get her bearings, and almost the first thing she saw was Kit leaning on the oars of the boat. "Where did you come from?" she demanded.

"I was snoozing in the boat when I saw you take off across the lake. I thought I'd follow to make sure you didn't get run down by a passing motorboat. There *are* some around, you know."

"Are there? I didn't see any." She was a little out of breath and was beginning to tire. "If you don't mind, I won't stay here chatting," she said pleasantly.

"Why don't you climb in? The water's cold and you've had quite enough of a swim for one day I should think."

He was right. It had been a longer swim than she had anticipated. "All right," she said and swam over to the side of the boat. She put her hands on the side. "I hope I don't swamp you."

"You won't." He moved to the far side of the boat to help balance it, and Mary pulled herself out of the water and into the rubber dinghy. She sat down and shook water out of her eyes. "Have a towel," he said hospitably, and gratefully she reached out and took it. She dried her face, pulled the elastic band out of her hair and began to towel it.

"I bit off more than I was ready to chew," she said candidly.

"You would have made it," he replied, moving back himself to the center of the boat.

"Oh, I know that. But I would have been tired. And then I would have had to go back." She finished toweling her hair and looked at him closely for the first time. He was wearing only bathing trunks, also navy, and around his neck hung a St. Joseph medal. She had given him that medal for his birthday four years ago. He caught the direction of her stare and his hand went up to finger the medal. "I still have it," he said. "I don't know if I really believe in it, but I've always worn it. It's about all I've got left of you."

Her eyes dropped. "Don't, Kit," she said softly.
There was silence as the boat drifted and then she
said, "I hear Margot Chandler is to be your mother."

He laughed. "Isn't that a surprise? I suppose she's
getting too old for glamour-girl parts."

"Can she act?" Mary asked bluntly.

"It won't matter, I think," he replied thoughtfully.
"Gertrude is hardly a complex character. In fact, in
some ways she resembles many California women:
beautiful, loaded with sex appeal, essentially good-
natured, but shallow. I have a feeling all Margot
Chandler will need to do is play herself. She'll probably do very well. And the theater is small enough that
voice projection needn't be a problem."

Mary was silent for a minute, digesting what he had
just said. Then she smiled mischievously. "Eric Lindquist says that this production should be labeled "Hollywood Goes Arty."

Kit's answering smile was rueful. "He's exactly the
sort of kid I'd like to punch in the nose."

"I know," Mary answered longingly. "That boyish
grin . . ."

He began to row the boat toward the far side of the
lake. "You never did appreciate youthful male arro-
gance," he said. "You knocked it out of me fast
enough."

"You were never really arrogant," she said quietly.
"Just determined." She watched him row, watched the
smooth ripple of muscle across his arms and chest. He
was so slim that his impressive set of muscles always
came as something of a surprise. He had gotten them
working in a warehouse, he once told her. It had been
one of the many jobs that put him through school.

The boat was almost on the shore and Mary noticed, with surprise, a strip of sand along the water's edge. "I didn't know there was a beach here."

"I noticed it yesterday and I thought I'd take a look. I don't think it's private property—there's no dock or boat at any rate."

Mary had been brought up on the shore of Long Island Sound and a beach always beckoned to her. Kit jumped out of the boat into waist-high water and she followed without hesitation. They towed the boat to shore and walked out onto the sand.

"This has been put here by someone," she said, wriggling her toes luxuriously. "It's too fine to be native."

Kit was looking through the trees that surrounded the small sand crescent. "I think I see a house. It must be private property after all. I suppose we'd better go."

"Yes," she said regretfully. It was so peaceful and sheltered and quiet here. She walked back to the water and helped Kit push the boat out. He got in first and had reached out a hand to help her when a man with a camera jumped out from behind some trees on their left and began snapping furiously. Kit swore and made a motion to get out of the boat.

"No, don't!" Mary cried. She was in the boat by now. "Just push off. Please, Kit."

He hesitated a minute and then did as she asked, propelling the small dinghy with hard furious strokes away from the shore and the intruder.

"Goddamn parasites," he said. "Bloodsucking bastards." He was in a quiet, concentrated rage and his own fury served to dampen hers.

"It was a man called Jason Razzia," she said in a low shaking voice. "I met him this morning in town. He said he was doing a story about—us."

"Razzia," he said with loathing. "I know him. A free-lancer. The scrapings of a particularly rancid barrel. He's made me his pet project lately."

"Is it like this all the time?" she asked dazedly. "Don't they *ever* let you alone?"

"It's worse now than usual," he replied, a bitter twist to his mouth. "Most of the time, when I'm going about my work, they leave me alone. I have a house that's pretty well isolated out in a canyon, and photographers don't bother to camp at my door. It's you who are the interest now."

"Don't I know it," she returned even more bitterly. "All because you decided you had to play Hamlet at Yarborough."

"I wanted to play Hamlet," he said.

"You could very well have played Hamlet in California," she retorted.

He went on as if she had not interrupted. "And I wanted to see you again." He stopped rowing, rested his hands on the oars and looked at her. "Do you think the pursuit by media hounds is the worst part of living in California? Well it's not. The worst thing is the artificiality of so much of the place, the superficiality of so many of the people. Not everyone. There are some fine and talented people—people who are interested in doing good things. Like Mark Stevens, who directed my last film. But somehow I always have the strangest sensation of touching many people without being touched in turn myself." He smiled a little crookedly. "When I saw you again in May it was as if I had come home again."

It was exactly the feeling she had had when he kissed her, and his voicing it now jarred her unpleasantly. She frowned, not wanting to hear this, not wanting to respond to it. He was so clever, she thought. He knew just what to say to get to her. "You can't go home again," she said fiercely, staring at his feet. His toes were so straight. Hell, she thought, why did everything about him have to be so damn beautiful? She looked up into his face. "Thomas Wolfe wrote that many years ago, and it's true."

"Mary." He leaned forward and put a hand on her knee. "Listen to me, sweetheart . . ."

The sensations emanating from that lean brown hand reached all the way to her loins and stomach. "No!" she said violently. "Leave me alone!" And, precipitously, she dove off the boat and swam back to shore under the interested eyes of the assembled students.

She didn't linger on shore but slipped into her sandals, pulled her dress on over her wet suit, and headed for her cottage. This was the second day in a row she had fled from the lake because of Kit, she thought, as the screen door closed behind her. How on earth was she going to manage three weeks of this?

She was afraid of him. She was afraid of what the sight of him did to her, afraid of the memories his presence stirred in her mind and her heart and her body. It would be so easy, so fatally easy, to slip back into their old intimacy. It had happened this afternoon. When he had rowed her to that beach she hadn't murmured a protest. It had been so natural—

he had always been interested in exploring places he hadn't seen before and she had always gone along. When they had been at the cape. . . . God, she mustn't think of the cape.

She stripped off her wet suit and got into the shower. When she got out she put on a white terry-cloth bathrobe and went to lie on the bed. Why was she reacting this way, she asked herself desperately. Come on, she thought, you're supposed to be smart. You're not just a quivering mass of hormones; you're supposed to have a brain. Use it.

She stared at the ceiling and she thought. She thought of what he had said to her this afternoon and of how her hostility toward him dissipated the moment they were together again.

Together again. The last time they had been to-gether had been before he went to California. They had not had a long marriage, but it had been a deeply intimate one. She understood what he had said this af-ternoon about no one really touching him. She had felt that way too. Quite probably she was the single human being who knew him best in the world. In Cal-ifornia he would always feel he had to guard his tongue. He had not guarded it with her.

That was the problem. They had lived together so closely, had filled each other so completely—and then he had gone away. Except for that brief moment at the hospital she hadn't seen him again. All her bitter-ness had been directed at him in absentia. She had no experience of being around him and being hostile, or even indifferent. Her experience in being with him, the relationship she was so afraid of reprising here at Yar-borough, had been profoundly close and satisfying.

He had chosen the life he had, she thought stubbornly as she dressed. At one time she had been willing to share it with him, but no longer. No longer was she willing to give up her gentle world of literature, scholarship, and teaching. She was not willing to surrender her happiness—happiness based on security, familiarity, understanding, respect—for the harsh, publicity-hungry world of film, for marriage to a man she loved but did not trust. He had ridden roughshod over her once; she could not bear it if he ever did that to her again. No. Better to keep one's hand from the fire if one did not want to be burned.

The conversation at dinner was mainly about Margot Chandler and her amazing decision to come to Yarborough to play Gertrude. None of the professional cast had ever worked with her; they were mainly theater people and Margot Chandler's success had been solely in films.

"I've never met her," Kit offered at one point, "but I've heard she's inclined to be somewhat temperamental."

"Most big film stars are," said Alfred Block with a sneer. Mary looked at him closely. It really was a sneer.

"I didn't think anyone actually did that," she said in amazement. "I thought it only happened in books."

Everyone at the table looked puzzled, except Kit, who chuckled.

"Did what?" asked Frank wonderingly.

"Sneered," replied Mary. "He really did sneer. Curled his lip and everything. I thought it went out with Dickens."

George started to laugh and Alfred Block looked uncomfortable. "*Chris* certainly isn't temperamental," said Carolyn Nash both earnestly and adoringly.

"No, he's not," replied George, sobering. "Not that he can't be damn stubborn when it suits him." He stared across at his star who regarded him impeturbably in return.

"Too much stage business is distracting," Kit replied calmly. "I don't have to be constantly doing things in order to keep people watching me."

It was true and George knew it better than anyone. He smiled. "Stubborn," he repeated. "And—sometimes—right."

Mary kept to her plan of the evening before and stayed by George when they went into the recreation room. "You don't," she asked with tentative hopefulness, "happen to play bridge, do you?"

Melvin Shaw, the veteran English actor who was playing Polonius, jerked his head around. "Bridge?" he inquired. "Did someone mention bridge?"

"Yes," said Mary. "Do you play?"

He did. And so did George. And so—surprisingly—did one of the students who was working on costumes. She was an attractive no-nonsense girl who had impressed Mary in class with her intelligent questions; her name was Nancy Sealy.

The four settled down happily for the evening. Safe, thought Mary, as she raised George's bid by a heart. Kit did not play bridge. It was not one of the accomplishments highly valued in the Philadelphia neighborhood where he had grown up.

"I'll walk you home," George offered when the second rubber ended and Mary, remembering last night, accepted with a smile. Kit had left the rec room some time ago, but she couldn't be sure that he wasn't lying in wait for her somewhere on the path to her cottage.

She wasn't exactly free of him, however, as George apparently wanted to talk about his star. "Chris is a bit of an enigma, isn't he?" he said as they walked slowly up through the pines. He's not at all what I expected him to be."

"Oh?" said Mary.

"To be frank, I wasn't sure I wanted him. We've worked hard here to establish a reputation as the best summer theater in the country and I didn't want to risk it on the whim of a Hollywood star who fancied he could do Shakespeare."

"Why did you take him then?" Mary asked curiously.

"Timing, for one thing. When Adrian Saunders backed out I had to replace him fast."

"You could have gotten someone from the legitimate stage without too much difficulty."

She saw George's teeth gleam in the darkness. "Yeah. I know. I guess I just couldn't resist it."

"Having a superstar, you mean?"

"No. His voice. I just couldn't resist that voice. I went to see his last film again and that was what got me, that beautiful, flexible voice. He's the only American actor I know who really has the voice for Shakespeare. It seemed such a waste to hear it shouting 'Shoot, goddamn it'—which seemed to be his biggest line in that very unliterate film."

Mary laughed. "He did a lot of Shakespeare at drama school, George. I wouldn't worry."

"We're going to have every major critic in the country here for opening night, Mary," he said rather grimly. "As you said earlier, Chris isn't just an ordinary Hollywood actor. He isn't even an ordinary Hollywood star. He's a superstar. They'll be here to see if he really ought to be taken seriously or to see him fall on his face. It's his face, after all, that has been his ticket to success so far, not his acting."

"I always thought he was quite good in his films," Mary said quietly.

"He was. But they were hardly demanding."

"No, I suppose not." They had reached her cottage by now. "I have a bottle of Scotch tucked away," she said. "Would you like a nightcap?"

"Sounds good," he said, and came in after her. She got ice from the small refrigerator in the sitting room and poured two drinks. The night air was chilly on the porch so they sat down inside, Mary on the Early American sofa and George in a chair facing her.

"How are rehearsals going?" she asked, sipping her drink and drawing her legs up under her.

"Not bad at all. He won't fall on his face, if that's what you mean. He does know his stuff. In fact, I find him surprisingly professional."

"Why shouldn't he be professional?" she inquired frowningly.

"No reason. I suppose I thought he'd be rather the way he described Margot Chandler—temperamental. But he's not. And he has surprisingly little vanity. That probably amazed me most of all."

"He grew up in a tough Philadelphia neighborhood," said Mary with a small smile. "His looks were more a handicap than anything else. In order to hold his own he had to learn to do everything better than anyone else. And the two things they did in that neighborhood were fight and play basketball. He never learned to value his looks, that's for sure."

"Basketball?" said George on a note of inquiry.

"He went to Penn State on a basketball scholarship." She held her drink between her two palms and looked down into its amber depths. "He broke his thumb and was out for half the season in his sophomore year. That's when he tried out for a part in the college play. He got it and he was hooked. He threw up the basketball scholarship and went in for acting."

"I see," said George quietly. Then, unexpectedly, "You still wear his ring."

"Yes." A slight flush warmed her cheeks. "Technically we're still married. And a wedding ring is good protection."

"Hmm." George looked at her speculatively. "Half the women in this country would give their eyeteeth to be married to Chris Douglas."

"Well, I belong to the other half," she replied lightly.

"He still loves you. You must know that. He watches you all the time."

Unexpectedly she raised her eyes and he found himself thinking that he had never seen such utter blueness before; there was not a hint of gray or of green in those eyes. They were clear and darkly lashed and absolutely blue. "I know," she said tensely. "He follows me, too. And I don't want him to. I would never have come to Yarborough if I thought Kit was going to be here."

"Is that why you've been so attentive to me?" he asked wryly.

The blue gaze never wavered. "Yes," said Mary candidly. "I need protection."

"From your husband?"

She hesitated. "Yes," she repeated finally. "He is my husband, that's true. But we haven't lived together for over four years and I've told him I will never live with him again. If he wants a divorce he can have one. I just want him to leave me alone."

"I don't think he will, Mary," George said. "In fact, I think the main reason he came here was not to play Hamlet but to see you."

"I'm beginning to think so too." Mary suddenly felt very tired. "I was fool enough to tell him where I'd be for the summer, so I suppose part of it is my own fault."

"Why are you so afraid of him?" George asked innocently. "If you mean what you say, all you have to do is say no and keep on saying it. Chris can hardly kidnap you."

Mary sighed, put down her glass and stood up. "I suppose you're right. But sometimes I feel like King Canute standing on the sand and forbidding the tide to come in. Nothing that I say will make any difference." She smiled. "Good night, George."

"Good night, Mary. And thanks for the drink."

She stood at the screen door and watched him go off down the path. As she turned to go in the house she noticed a figure on the porch of the cottage next to hers. It was too dark to see anything but his outline but she knew he was watching her. Childishly she stuck her tongue out at him and slammed the cottage door as she went inside. Good God, she thought as she unzipped her skirt. I'm really regressing if I've descended to this. Wearily she undressed and went to bed.

Chapter Eight

❧

The next day Margot Chandler arrived at Yarborough. Mary first saw her at a cocktail reception George hastily threw together for the professional staff and the cast that afternoon. It was held in a lovely elegant old room in Avery Hall. Mary put on a white linen suit with a hot-pink blouse and walked uncomfortably on high heels down through the pines. She was frankly curious. She had only seen one or two of Margot Chandler's films, but over the course of the years, and the course of numerous husbands, the star had become something of a national institution. She represented, to Mary's mind, The Hollywood World. What would she be like?

She was, to begin with, exquisite. Small and delicately made, she wore a simple black dress that Mary realized must have cost the earth. She may have been forty-five but she most certainly did not look it. Her pale hair was soft and shining, her skin was fresh and unlined, her figure slim and flexible. "Good heavens," said Mary, as she was introduced by George, "no one is ever going to believe you're Hamlet's *mother*."

The perfect Chandler teeth showed in a charming smile. "I was a child bride, of course." she said delicately. Kit was standing next to her and she raised her famous green eyes to his face. "I don't think I had expected such a large son, though." The top of her blond head came only to his shoulder. She put her hand on his arm. "Darling, I should so like to introduce you to my secretary. He is a great admirer of your films and is quite *longing* to meet you." She cast a brief smile in Mary and George's direction before she deftly steered Kit off toward another corner of the room.

"Well," said Mary in some amusement as she watched the small feminine figure tow Kit's six feet three skillfully away. "So that's Margot Chandler. It was a brief meeting, of course, but most interesting."

George chuckled. "God help me. I have to direct her."

"Darling," Mary purred, putting her arm on his sleeve and looking up at him through her lashes. "Would you mind terribly getting me a drink?"

"Cut it out," said George inelegantly. They walked together toward the table that had been set up as a bar. "She's not living on campus, you know. Too terribly rustic."

"Oh dear. Where is she staying?"

"The Stafford Inn. It's the poshest place in the area. Not posh at all by her standards of course—she called it 'rather a hole,'—but the best we can do locally."

Mary sipped her drink and smiled absently at

Adam Truro, the boy who was playing Horatio. "Will she be eating with us?"

"Tonight she is," George replied. "Somehow I rather doubt that the college cuisine is going to be up to her standard, but I did emphasize our atmosphere of family coziness here at Yarborough."

"I'll bet she's just going to love it," Mary said dryly and George made a comic face.

Margot Chandler did in fact accompany them to the dining room that evening. The meal was roast chicken with gravy, mashed potatoes, and peas. She looked at it with wide-eyed incredulity. "Darling," she said reproachfully to George, "I can't eat this. Think of the calories."

"I'm sorry, Margot," said George. "I suppose the food here is rather caloric. The kitchen staff is used to cooking for hungry youngsters, I'm afraid."

"Perhaps I'll just have a word with the chef," Margot murmured gently and disappeared in the direction of the kitchen. When she returned it was with a white-uniformed waiter who removed her plate. She reseated herself and smiled seraphically around the table.

Kit, who was already halfway through his dinner, said with amusement, "Are they fixing you something else?"

"Yes. The chef, such a dear man—he speaks only Spanish you know—quite understood my problem." The chef apparently did, for shortly thereafter he appeared himself carrying a new plate that contained a grilled steak with a beautiful salad on the side. The Chandler eyes flashed in gratitude and Mary watched

in some awe as the chef nearly fell over himself pro-
testing to her that in the future he would be
pleased—ecstatic actually—to cook for her whatever
she might desire. Margot answered in lovely liquid
Spanish and the chef departed with a magestic flour-
ish. Dinner resumed.

"I've admired you for years, Miss Chandler," said
Eric Lindquist with a charming boyish smile. He had
maneuvered successfully to be at the same table with
The Star.

"Have you?" Margot looked speculatively for a
minute at Eric's handsome, suntanned face. She
smiled. "I'm sorry, I'm afraid I've forgotten your
name."

"Eric Lindquist," he said. The admiration in his
blue eyes was blatant. "I'm playing Fortinbras."

"Oh, yes." She took a dainty bite of her steak and
turned to Kit. "I'm counting so much on you, Chris
darling, to get me through this play. The thought of
my own daring quite terrifies me." She gazed up at
him out of wide and helpless eyes. It was quite clear
that Eric Lindquist held no interest for her and for the
remainder of the meal she skillfully, charmingly, and
mercilessly monopolized Kit's attention.

Mary said little but watched thoughtfully as Margot
went into action. When they all went into the rec
room after dinner, she found herself alone with Margot for a minute as George and Kit went to get them
coffee. Margot looked at Mary speculatively, taking
her in from the top of her black head to the tips of her
patent-leather pumps. "You're married to Chris?" she
asked bluntly.

Mary felt her temper rising. She did not like that look at all. "Yes," she said shortly.

"But you don't live together?"

"No."

"I see." Margot smiled at her charmingly. "You are a teacher here, I understand."

"That is correct, Miss Chandler."

The men returned and George handed Mary her cup. Margot smiled dazzlingly at the two males and said, "Isn't it just marvelous, a woman intelligent enough to teach college. You must be very smart, Mary."

Mary smiled back even more dazzlingly. "Yes," she said, "I am."

"She graduated summa cum laude," said Kit, deadpan, and Mary shot him a look.

The Chandler nose wrinkled. "Summa cum . . . What does that mean?"

"It means that Mary is very smart indeed," said George with a smile.

"Mary, George." It was Melvin Shaw's English accents. "How about some bridge?"

"Wonderful," said Mary with alacrity. In Melvin she had tapped a deadly serious bridge player—he even had Master's points, he had told them last night. She saw he had Nancy Sealy in tow. "George?" he asked again.

George cast a quick look at Margot and Kit. She looked smooth as cream; he looked a trifle grim and the dark eyes that looked back at George held a definite message. "Isn't there someone else who could make a fourth?" George asked Melvin.

"No. No one who can play worth a damn."

"Oh, well in that case . . ." George allowed himself to be towed off, casting an apologetic glance back at Kit, who looked like thunder. Margot immediately put a hand on his arm and began to talk to him.

As Mary sat down at the card table she involuntarily glanced over to where her husband stood with Margot. They made a striking couple, her small, feminine fairness against his towering male darkness. But no matter how delicate and fragile she might appear on the surface, Mary was sure that underneath Margot was a cool, tough customer. She looked closer to thirty than forty, but her sophistication and assurance came from years of power, years of handling men to her own advantage. She seemed to be handling Kit very well. The scowl was gone and he was laughing. After a few minutes they left the room together.

"Mary" said Melvin in exasperation as she played a card. "That was my queen. You just trumped your own partner."

"Oh dear," said Mary, trying to recall her wandering wits. "Sorry, Mel. I wasn't paying attention."

"Well, please do so," he said severely.

"Yes, I'll try." And she stared resolutely at her hand.

For the next two days Mary scarcely saw Kit, George, Alfred, or Margot. "Hell," George had muttered to her as their paths crossed briefly on Friday, "she doesn't even know her lines. And she needs her hand held constantly. I'm going to tear my hair out."

The fact that Margot was proving a disrupting force among the cast was confirmed by Carolyn Nash, who sat down next to Mary at the lakefront on Saturday afternoon. "She's a pain in the neck," said Carolyn forthrightly in answer to Mary's question as to how Margot was doing. "She hangs on Chris like a leech, and every time George moves her off center stage she cries."

"Oh God," said Mary. "What a mess. But is she any good, Carolyn?"

"I don't know," the girl grumbled. Then, unwillingly: "She may be all right. Chris has been coaching her about her voice. It's a little thin and high." She sighed. "He's incredibly patient with her. I'd like to give her a good swift kick myself."

"Yes, well you aren't a man," Mary murmured.

"That's true. She's very beautiful."

"Very."

They looked at each other and laughed ruefully. "I must say," confessed Mary, "that I really didn't believe women like that existed. I thought it was all part of the Hollywood myth. She actually calls people 'darling.' "

"She lays it on so thick you can't believe it," said Carolyn in amazement. "I mean, I admire Chris enormously. I think he's wonderful, actually. But she . . ."

"I know. She makes Scarlett O'Hara look subtle." They both laughed again and felt much better for having shared their mutual dislike of La Belle Chandler, as Mary called her nastily. They neither of them bothered to reflect that Margot's chief sin in both their eyes was that since she had arrived, she had totally monopolized Christopher Douglas.

Sunday morning Mary arose early and decided to go to Mass first and have breakfast afterwards. She put on her blue shirt-dress and espadrilles and got in the car. It was the first time she had ventured off campus since Wednesday when she had been accosted by Jason Razzia. She looked cautiously around as she drove out of the college gate but there was no one around. She made it to church without incident and on the way back to college stopped to pick up the Sunday papers. The store she stopped at was a small food market that had a lunch counter as well where they served coffee, donuts, and sandwiches. Sitting at the counter having a cup of coffee was her nemesis. Razzia jumped up the minute he saw her.

"Hi there, Mrs. Douglas! You and Chris done any more boating? Or has Margot Chandler been keeping him too busy?" Mary ignored him and went to the cash register to pay for her papers and the few groceries she had picked up. "She's between husbands right at present, you know, and may be in the market for a younger man. It seems to be the new fad."

Mary gritted her teeth, collected her change, and stalked to the door. "You're a good-looking dame," came the revolting voice from behind her, "but Margot is supposed to be pure dynamite. Better watch out."

Mary longed, with a passion that curled her fingers, to turn and smash him across his hateful face. She climbed into her car and relieved her feelings slightly by slamming the door hard and pretending that Jason's Razzia's fingers were in the way.

She got back to college, to safety, she thought as she drove in the gates and went to have breakfast in the dining room. She took her papers along, and over her second cup of coffee she opened the theater sec-

tion of the *Times*. The headline jumped out at her:
CHRISTOPHER DOUGLAS TACKLES HAMLET. She put
down her coffee cup, folded the paper, and read:

During the past ten years some of the most interesting and daring of our theatrical ventures have
come out of Yarborough College's Summer
Drama Festival. Last year George Clark, the festival's talented and innovative director, sent on
to Broadway a very smart and excruciatingly
funny production of Sheridan's eighteenth-cen-
tury classic *The School for Scandal*. Two years
before we had Louis Murray and Merrill Kane in
a very fine and passionate *Antigone*, a play that
was distinguished by Mr. Clark's excellent use of
the chorus. This year, with a piece of casting that
takes one's breath away, Mr. Clark is presenting
Christopher Douglas in *Hamlet*.

Hamlet is perhaps Shakespeare's most fascinating and demanding character. The actor who por-
trays Hamlet places himself in a position of inevitable comparison to the great actors of our
century: John Gielgud, Laurence Olivier, and
Richard Burton to name a few. The challenge is
daunting. Mr. Douglas first of all is an American, and no no American actor in recent
memory has risen to the challenge of Shakespeare in any way comparable to the British.
Secondly, Mr. Douglas's main experience has
been in movies. He had stage experience as a
student, and was in fact given his first screen test
on the basis of a performance at New Haven's

Long Stage, but the fact remains that the greater part of his career has been spent in films.

It has been a phenomenally successful career, one hastens to add. There is not another screen actor performing today who can equal his popularity. His films invariably make back their initial investment in the first month of showing. But is that admittedly astonishing record enough to enable him to undertake so demanding a role as Hamlet?

One's immediate reaction is to say no. No, the man who starred in *Raid on Kailis,* that glossy, adventurous blockbuster, is not the man who can play Hamlet. Which is not to say that Mr. Douglas was not very fine in his last film. He was. He has a screen presence that is possibly unsurpassed by any other actor in recent memory: a really beautiful face in the classic sense, a lean and splendid body and a voice that most actors would sell their souls for. Perhaps that is the problem, perhaps he has so much going for him that it is too easy for him to sit back and let the façade do all the work.

And yet . . . one remembers Ivan of *The Russian Experiment.* It was his first role and his best, and hinted at possibilities within him yet to be explored. In his recent films he has portrayed the popular modern hero: casual on the surface, tough and self-sufficient underneath. He has done it charmingly, effortlessly, and has managed at the same time to convey a sexual quality that is remarkable considering the restraint of most of his love scenes. But in Ivan we had something more: a depth and complexity hinted at, but palpable. The man who played Ivan *may* be able to do Hamlet.

Mr. Douglas apparently thinks himself that it is time he moved on from the world of popular movies into something more challenging. He could not, however, have picked a more formidable role. One applauds his courage. And awaits the outcome.

There was the sound of a chair being pulled out and Mary looked up to see Kit sitting down with a cup of coffee. "Have you seen the *Times?*" she asked immediately.

"No, I haven't." He sipped his coffee. "Good morning."

She wrinkled her nose slightly. "Sorry. Good morning. And read this article." She handed it over and picked up her own cup, her eyes on his face as he read. When he had finished he put it down and looked thoughtful.

"I don't know what whim brought you to Yarborough, my friend, but you've put yourself behind the eight ball, haven't you?" she said tensely.

"Have I?" he replied calmly.

"Yes. George said the first-night audience would be packed with critics waiting to see if you were going to fall on your face. Apparently he was right." She tapped the paper with a long, nervous finger.

"Everything Calder said here is true, you know. I did coast through my last three movies. It was all I had to do, really." His eyes were black and inscrutable as he watched her face.

"I know." She looked at him very seriously. "Why did you take those parts, Kit? They surprised me. I thought, after *The Russian Experiment*, you would hold out for something more serious."

"Can't you guess?"

"No."

He smiled crookedly. "Money, my dear. Filthy lucre. I wanted to put enough of it in the bank so that I'd never have to worry about it again. And I've done that. I had ten percent of *Raid On Kailis,* you know." He pushed his coffee cup away. "I'm not ashamed of those films. They were well done, they were fun, they were exciting without being violent. They weren't terribly serious, I'll agree, but they served a purpose. They entertained millions."

"Yes," she said slowly. "I know that." She gave him a worried look. "But you are going to have to come up with a helluva Hamlet to beat the image you've made for yourself. The critics won't incline toward leniency."

"Are you concerned about me, Mary?" he asked softly.

"Yes. I am. The rehearsal time is too short. You're working with students. And Margot." Her voice altered imperceptibly as she said that last name and he grinned.

"She's going to be all right. All George has to do is put her at center stage and she's happy."

"How about you?"

He looked sardonic. "I don't need the center of the stage."

Her throat was suddenly dry. "Kit"—unconsciously she leaned toward him—"can you do it?"

"I think so. If I want to." His voice was soft and very deep. "Is it important to you that I succeed?"

"Yes." Her voice in return was barely a whisper. "Yes, it is."

"Mind if I join you?" said George's cheerful voice.

"Of course not," returned Mary after a minute, forcing a smile.

Kit turned his splendid raven head toward George and favored him with a cold stare. "You're up late," he said disapprovingly.

"It's Sunday," replied George mildly, tucking into his plate of scrambled eggs. "My day of rest."

"Why don't you go over and hold Margot's hand for a while?" asked Kit disagreeably.

"It's not my hand she wants to hold." George refused to be ruffled by his star's evident bad temper. Kit gave up trying to intimidate him and turned to Mary.

"How about a game of tennis?" he asked.

"Tennis?" She looked at him incredulously. "You never played tennis before. You said it was a sissy game."

He grinned a little. "I was being defensive. I didn't want you to teach me to play because I knew you'd beat me."

She gave him a long blue stare. "And now you think I can't?"

"I don't know," he returned frankly, "but at least it'll be a contest."

"I'll meet you at the courts in half an hour," she said.

"Fine." He smiled pleasantly at George. "See you later," he said and strolled casually out of the dining room. Everyone present, including George and Mary, watched him go.

Half an hour later, dressed in a white tennis dress and carrying her racquet and a Thermos, Mary arrived at the tennis courts. There were four of them, each with a concrete rubberized surface and all four were presently in use. Mary went to sit next to Kit on the bench and looked at him appraisingly. He was wearing white shorts and a light blue shirt.

"How good are you?" she asked speculatively.

He glanced sideways down at her, his lowered lashes looking absurdly long against the hard male line of his cheek. "You'll find out."

"We're through now," said Nancy Sealy as she came over to the bench with the girl she had been playing. "You can have our court, Mary."

"Thanks." Mary flashed the girl a smile and bent her head to unzip her racquet cover. That look of Kit's had disturbed her, and as she took the court she tried to ignore the suddenly accelerated beat of her heart.

They warmed up for five minutes, then Kit said, "Shall we start? You can serve first."

"Okay." She put one ball in the pocket of her dress, picked up another, and went to stand at the service line. Mary had been playing tennis since she was eight years old. Her parents belonged to a golf and tennis club and she had always spent hours every summer on the courts. She wasn't a powerful player, but she was extremely steady and accurate. She tossed the ball high in the air and served. Kit returned it deep to the baseline with a hard forehand shot. Mary, who had moved in, missed it. She stood for a minute looking at him in surprise, then went to serve again. This time she put it on his backhand side and his return, while deep, was not as hard. She sent it back with her own smooth, classic forehand and eventually took the point.

She eventually took the game as well, but it took three deuces before she was able to put it away. Then Kit moved to the service line.

The ball boomed across the net and was by her before she had finished getting her racquet back. "Good grief," she said. "What was that?"

"Was it in?" he asked.

"What I could see of it was."

"Good." He grinned. "My problem is that all too often it isn't."

It was an extremely strenuous set. Kit made up in power what he lacked in accuracy and Mary's wrist was aching from returning his shots. It took them an hour to reach 6-6.

"Shall we play a tie breaker?" he asked as he came to the net to hand her the balls.

"Why don't we quit now?" she replied. "That way we both win."

"We neither of us win, you mean," he contradicted.

She made an exasperated face. "You're so bloody competitive. All right, we'll play a tie breaker."

"No." Unexpectedly he put the balls in his pocket. "No, you're right. We'll quit while we're both ahead."

"I'm dying of thirst," she confessed as they walked off the court together. They had been playing in the full sun and her face and hair were damp with sweat. She looked at Kit and saw that his shirt was soaked. "I brought a jug of water with me," she said, gesturing to the Thermos tucked under the bench. "I'll share it with you."

They sat down together on the bench in the shade and Mary poured the water. She had only one cup so she drank first, refilled it, and passed it to him. "You always think of everything," he said as he accepted the cup.

"Well, I've been playing tennis for a lot longer than you. If you ever get more consistency on that first serve, though, you'll make mincemeat of me. It's vicious."

"Yeah. When it goes in."

"You're not missing by much. You just need more practice. You could use a little more work on your backhand too."

"Mmm."

She hooked several wet tendrils of hair behind her ears and smiled ruefully. "My wrist hurts. It was like returning cannonballs."

He didn't answer for a minute and she poured herself some more water. She could feel his eyes on her. "What we need is a swim," he said at last. "What do you say?"

She thought of the cool clear lake. "I say that sounds good."

"Great." He stood up and picked up both their racquets and the water jug. "Let's go change into bathing suits."

"Okay." She fell into step beside him, her own long lithe stride almost the equal of his. A little voice inside her said she oughtn't to be spending time with him like this, that it was dangerous. Nonsense, said Mary silently to that uncomfortable little voice. There will be a million people around the lakefront. How can it possibly be dangerous?

They didn't go to the school lakefront. When she came out of her cottage dressed in a suit and terry-cloth cover-up, she found Kit sitting on her front steps. He wore bathing trunks and an ancient gray college sweat shirt that she recognized. "Good God," she said before she thought. "Do you still have that thing? I should have thought you'd have some designer sportswear by now."

"There's nothing wrong with this sweat shirt," he returned amiably. "There aren't any holes in it, are there?"

"No." She smiled at him, unaware of the affectionate amusement in her eyes. "In some ways you haven't changed at all. You never did give a damn about clothes."

"I like them clean and comfortable. As long as they meet those two requirements, I'm satisfied." They had begun walking down through the woods and at this point he veered off into the pines. "I've found a nice spot on the lake—a little cove. It's on college property so we won't be trespassing. Come on."

"But Kit," she protested as he plunged off through the trees. "I don't want to . . ."

He stopped and turned. "For God's sake, stop acting like a nun about to be raped. Come on!"

"Don't be crude," she snapped in return, but she followed him off the path and down through the woods. After about five minutes they came out of the trees and there they were on the shore of the lake. "Oh Kit," she breathed. "It's lovely."

"Great for fishing," he said with satisfaction. "I was out here at five this morning and it was beautiful."

"Did you catch anything?"

"You'll be eating it for dinner," he replied with a grin.

He dropped his towel and stripped his sweat shirt off. She began to do the the same. "Daddy certainly made a convert out of you," she said, her voice muffled by her cover-up as she pulled it over her head. "Nothing, but nothing, would get me out of bed at five in the morning."

"Does your father still have the boat?"

"Yes." She looked away from him to the sparkling lake water. Kit had loved to go out with her father on those early-morning fishing expeditions. She had thought sometimes that he enjoyed her father so much because he had never really known his own.

"Race you in," he said.

"Okay." They both headed for the lake at a run and their diving bodies went into the water at almost the same instant. The two sleek black heads emerged close together and they yelped simultanously, "It's freezing!" The lake here dropped off steeply after the first few feet, and though they were not far from shore, Mary found she was over her head. She treaded water and looked around.

They were in a small cove, protected from the college waterfront by a promontory of pine trees. Mary could hear some of the students shouting and laughing as they played volleyball, but they were hidden from her view, as she was hidden from theirs.

They swam for perhaps ten minutes and then, by unspoken mutual consent, headed back to the shore. Mary picked up her towel and silently watched Kit as he dried himself vigorously. He was not watching her, he was looking off down the lake, and so she let her eyes linger on the smooth brown expanse of muscled shoulders and back, the strong brown column of his neck. He finished drying himself and spread out the towel on the patch of grass that grew beyond the trees. He lay down, put his hands behind his head, and closed his eyes against the sun. "Tell me about Hamlet," he said.

She spread her own towel next to his, sat down and rummaged in her canvas bag for a comb. "What do you want to know?"

"I find him hard to figure out. He vacillates so— one moment he's full of energy, vowing to avenge his father's murder, and the next he's in a blue funk, unable to do anything at all."

Slowly she combed the tangles out of her wet hair. "That's the Hamlet problem in a nutshell. It's not the typical Elizabethan revenge tragedy at all. The conflict in *Hamlet* is within the hero, not outside him."

"As I understand it," Kit said, "according to the code of the revenge tragedy, Hamlet is supposed to murder his uncle because he's discovered that his uncle murdered his father. An eye for an eye and all that. And he doesn't seem to question the morality of the code. He seems to think he ought to murder his uncle. God knows, he has reason enough to hate him.

Aside from killing Hamlet's father, he's stolen the throne from Hamlet and married his adored mother. Hamlet keeps *saying* he hates Claudius, that he wants to kill him, but every time he has a chance, he flubs it."

Mary finished with her hair and returned the comb to her bag. "Haven't you talked about this with George?"

"Yes. He's inclined toward the Olivier interpretation, that Hamlet's feelings for his mother are what get in the way. But I think there's something more."

Mary wrapped her arms around her knees. "He's a terribly complicated character," she said slowly. "He doesn't know himself why he is incapable of acting. I think it stems from his state of mind, myself."

"The first soliloquy, you mean.

> Oh God! God!
> How weary, stale, flat, and unprofitable
> Seem to me all the uses of the world!

Kit's beautiful voice lingered on the words, drawing out all the vowel sounds in a way that sent a sudden shiver down her spine.

"Precisely," she said after a minute's silence. "What is the point of acting in such a world? It won't bring his father back, it won't make his mother chaste, it won't restore the innocence of his love for Ophelia. Yet consciously he feels he *must* act. The contradiction puts a terrible strain on his mind."

"He can be a nasty bastard."

"Yes. He's dangerously close to the edge at times.

And yet, there is a basic beauty and goodness about him that shines through all the torment."

"Hmm. I can see why he's considered such a challenge."

"The ultimate challenge for an actor, it's said." She turned a little to look at him. "Are you afraid, Kit?"

His eyes remained closed. "Yes," he said. "To do it well I'm going to have to reveal myself as I've never done before. Yes, you could say I'm afraid."

She didn't say anything but kept looking at his quiet relaxed face. She had told him he hadn't changed, but that wasn't true. There were faint lines at the corners of his eyes and a look about his mouth that hadn't been there before. He looked older. He looked as if he had suffered. She was conscious of deep surprise as she thought this and his eyes opened and looked into hers. "Lie down here with me," he said softly, and her heart began to hammer in her breast.

Chapter Nine

"No," she said. She dragged her eyes away from his and turned so her back was to him. "If you start that, I'll leave."

"Will you?" He reached up and caught her arm, levering her back with the strength of his wrist until she was lying beside him on the spread towels. In a minute he had rolled over and pinned her down, his mouth coming down on hers in a hard, hungry kiss whose intensity pressed her head back against the striped towel and into the ground. At the touch of his mouth all her defenses melted. She was hardly aware of when the tenseness left her body and her mouth answered to the demand of his.

"Mary." His voice was a husky murmur in her ear. "I love you. Don't you know that?"

"Do you, Kit?" She looked up into his face so close above her own. "I don't know what I know anymore," she said and lightly ran her finger over his cheekbone.

He bent his head and kissed her throat. "Come back to California with me."

She closed her eyes. The urge to give in to him was tremendous. "I can't," she whispered. "It isn't my kind of world, it never could be."

"You can bring your own world with you," he said and sat up.

At his withdrawal she felt alone and bereft. After a minute she opened her eyes to gaze up at him. "What do you mean?"

"I mean there are universities in California—damn good ones too. Why couldn't you teach at one of them?"

"Teach?" she said weakly.

"Yes. Or write. Isn't that what you like to do best? Your book was excellent—as I'm sure you know."

Her eyes widened. "You read my book?"

His eyes were smiling at her. "You saw my movies."

"Yes." How could such dark eyes look so softly tender? She sat up and leaned her forehead on her knees. "You'd want me to go on teaching?"

"Of course I want you to go on teaching!" He sounded almost violent. "I've always wanted you to fulfill your potential. I would never stop you from doing that. That's why I was so upset when—when you said you would give up your fellowship."

He had shied away from mentioning the baby and she too avoided touching that particular pain. "I don't know, Kit. It's too hard to combine careers. I've seen it happen over and over again. Someone's always got to give."

Her hair had begun to dry in the sun and a strand of it swung forward over her cheek. He reached out and gently pushed it back off her face. "If you like," he said, "I'll move east."

Her eyes were great blue pools in her clear, fine-boned face. "Do you mean that?"

"Yes. I don't think I could manage Massachusetts. I'd have to be closer to New York. Maybe Connecticut again if you want to stay in New England."

"I don't know," she said again and heard the uncertainty in her own voice.

"Will you think about it?"

"I—yes."

He smiled at her. "Good girl." He rose to his feet and held a hand out to her. "Time for lunch," he said lightly, and she put her hand in his and let him pull her to her feet. "Your nose if red," he said as he picked up the towels.

"Rats. My sunscreen is in my bag. I forgot to put it on." She peered at her shoulders. "I'm really not the California type, Kit."

"I'll build you a screened-in porch," he said. "Come on."

"All right," she answered irritably, annoyed by his haste. "What's the big rush? Are you *that* hungry?"

"Yes, I am." He looked at her, a wicked gleam in his dark eyes. "But not for food. If we stay here any longer, you'll find out what I *am* hungry for."

"I'm coming," she said quickly and picked up her bag.

He raised an eyebrow but said only, "Follow me, Stanley," as he walked into the pines.

Her nose *was* red and so were her shoulders. She decided to make herself a peanut-butter-and-jelly sandwich and spend the afternoon on her porch reading the papers. It was difficult, however, to concentrate on the problems of the Middle East and Latin America. The problems of Mary O'Connor Douglas seemed so much more urgent.

She had told him she would consider going back to him. She couldn't believe she had said that, but she had. She had meant it too. She must be insane.

Of course he hadn't meant what he said about coming east. She knew Kit too well. His career came first with him; he had only said that to get under her guard. And he had got under her guard—damn him.

Part of her longed for him, longed for him and ached with missing him. And part of her feared him, feared what would happen if he turned away from her again as he had once before. She didn't know if she could dare to risk it again.

At about four o'clock George appeared at her door and she invited him in for a drink. He left at five and she went in to change for dinner. There had been no sign of Kit all afternoon and she found herself looking forward to seeing him at dinner.

He wasn't there. Nor was Margot Chandler.

"Where are Chris and Margot?" Carolyn Nash asked George, and Mary could have kissed her for her bluntness.

"Chris went over to the Stafford Inn this afternoon to work with her," George replied calmly. "I expect they're having dinner there."

"Just who is the director around here, George?"
Alfred Block asked insultingly. "Ever since the Queen
Bee arrived it seems as if Chris is taking over. *He* tells
her what to do, how to stand, how to speak."

"That's true," put in Eric Lindquist. He gave
George a sunshiny smile. "I haven't liked to say anything, but . . ."

"You creeps!" said Carolyn indignantly. "It isn't
Chris's fault if she hangs on him like a parasite. He's
only thinking of the good of the production."

Mary was startled and a little alarmed. She had no
idea there was such discord in the ranks. She looked
at George, who did not seem the least perturbed by
what was being said. He looked so high-strung and
nervous, she thought, that his calm was a perpetual
surprise to her. He said now, pleasantly but firmly, "*I*
am the director of this play, no one else. And I have a
leading lady to deal with who is extremely nervous
about her first stage role. She will do very well if only
we can instill some confidence in her. Chris is the person who has had the most success doing that, and I
am grateful to him for his effort. But when it comes
down to what happens on that stage, I am in charge.
And I would suggest that none of you forget it." He
went back to eating his dinner.

Mary looked at him in admiration. He glanced her
way, caught her look, and winked. She smiled a little
in return and pushed some food around on her plate.
She wasn't hungry. The idea of Kit and Margot together quite took her appetite away.

They played cards after dinner. If nothing else,
Mary thought, this summer will have improved my

bridge game. By ten o'clock she had a headache, however, and excused herself to go to bed. Melvin Shaw, who hated to see the best player after himself disappear, protested. But she rose, said firmly, "Good night, Melvin," and prepared to leave.

"Shall I see you to your cottage?" George asked.

"No. I really am tired and headachy," she said. "I'll see you tomorrow."

"It's probably the coming storm that's put you out of sorts," said Nancy Sealy. "It's amazing how the weather affects one."

"Is there a storm coming?" asked Mary sharply.

"There's supposed to be," the girl replied. "I heard it on the radio before I came down to dinner."

"Oh," said Mary faintly. "I see. Well, good night everyone."

The night was cool as she stepped out into the darkness, and there *was* the feel of a storm. Mary hurried up the path, anxious to reach the shelter of her cottage. Kit's windows were dark and his car was gone.

Once she was inside she undressed quickly and got into bed. She felt strung-up and tense. There was going to be a thunderstorm. She knew it, could feel it, and hated it.

When she was fourteen years old, Mary and a friend had been walking home from the tennis courts when a sudden thunderstorm had come up. They were taking a shortcut across a field and the lightning had been terrifying, shooting in jagged bolts from the sky. Mary had been frightened, but she remembered what her father had once said about getting caught on a golf course in a thunderstorm. "We should lie down flat!" she shouted to her girl friend.

"Yuck. The ground is soaked," her friend had replied. "I'm going to run for it."

The sky had lighted up. "Not me," said Mary, who had great faith in her father's wisdom. She had dropped to the ground as the other girl began to run across the field. A bolt of lightning had been attracted by the upright, running figure. The girl had been killed instantly, and ever since then Mary had been petrified by thunderstorms.

It didn't actually begin until about midnight. There was distant rumbling for about half an hour and then it started to rain. A bolt of lightning lit up the night outside Mary's window and a few seconds later came a sharp crack of thunder.

Wrapped in a blanket, she crawled out of bed and went to hide in the corner of her bedroom. She was huddled there, shaking uncontrollably, when she heard a voice from the sitting room calling her name. She tried to answer but a crack of thunder drowned her out. Her bedroom door opened and Kit stood there, dressed in jeans, and a sweat shirt. He saw her almost immediately. "Oh, sweetheart," he said gently. He crossed the room and sat down on the floor beside her. "You're perfectly safe, you know. If it hits anything it'll be one of the trees, not the cottage."

"I-I know," she stuttered, turning with a great rush of gratitude into the warm safety of his arms. "But somehow knowing doesn't seem to help."

He held her closely, drawing her into the shelter of his body, knowing from past experience that this more than his words would comfort her. She closed her eyes and pressed against him, not even noticing the wetness of his shirt under her cheek.

The storm lasted for about twenty minutes, during which time they stayed huddled together on the floor. Then it began to abate, the thunder sounding more distant, the lightning flashes less bright. Finally all that was left was the rain, beating steadily against the roof and the windows.

"It's all over," said Kit's voice gently.

"Yes." Her tense, cramped muscles relaxed a little. She tried to laugh. "I feel so stupid, but I can't seem to help it."

"I know." His hand was moving slowly, caressingly, up and down her back. His cheek was against her hair. She closed her eyes and rested against him.

"You knew I'd be a basket case." It was a statement not a question.

"Yes. I thought I'd better come over and check on you. It was a nasty storm."

"Mmm." It wasn't fear she was feeling now but something else. His hand continued its smooth rhythmic stroking and she drew a deep uneven breath.

"Mary," he said and she looked up. He bent his head and began to kiss her, a deep, slow, profoundly erotic kiss. She lay back in his arms, her head against his shoulder, her arms coming up to circle his neck. His lips moved from her mouth to bury themselves in her neck. His hand slid under her pajama top and cupped her breast. "Mary," he muttered, "my princess, my Irish rose . . ."

The love words, the touch of his mouth, his hand,

shattered whatever resistance she had left. "Let's get into bed," he murmured.

Her will to deny him had totally left her; she felt herself giving up, giving way. "All right," she whispered, and he got to his feet, pulling her up with him. He picked her up and laid her on the bed and stood beside it for a minute as he stripped his shirt off and undid the buckle of his jeans. She had left a lamp on and she watched him in its dim glow. Then he was beside her, his long fingers undoing the buttons of her pajama top, going to the elastic at her waist.

He touched her bared flesh and she felt him as a flame of desire, a flame that burned deep within her; and deep within her rose the urge to answer him, to satisfy him, to give to him and hold nothing back for herself. "Kit," she whispered, and he kissed her again, his long lean body hard and heavy now on hers. Her own body remembered the feel of him all too well, and quite suddenly she wanted him as badly as he wanted her. There was no one like him, nothing else in the world like this. "Kit," she said, urgently now, and then "Ah . . . h," as he buried himself deep within her. She shuddered as the piercing, quivering, throbbing tension began to mount within her. Her fingers were pressed deep into his back, white with pressure.

"Mary, baby, love." As one they moved together in profound, shuddering, ecstatic passion.

Afterward she was utterly still, lying quiet under the weight of his body, and he was still with her. After a long time he stirred and shifted his position. "I'm too heavy for you."

"No," she said. "You're not."

He looked down at her with dark, warm, peaceful eyes. "Go to sleep, Princess." he said, and turned her over on her side, the way she liked to sleep, and pulled her into the warmth of his body. She closed her eyes and in two minutes was deeply asleep.

Mary woke early the next morning to the sound of the birds. She turned to find Kit lying beside her, his chin propped on his hands, his brow lightly furrowed. He turned his head slightly when he heard her move and his eyes, meeting hers, were uncertain and wary.

He had taken advantage of the situation last night and he was evidently unsure of what her reaction would be in the clear light of the morning after. If I had half a brain, Mary thought, I'd tell him to get out. She felt her lips curving in a smile. "I knew I'd be like King Canute," she said.

His face dissolved into laughter. "Why King Canute?"

"He was the fellow who ordered the tide not to come in."

He was still laughing. "God, Mary, I love you. There isn't another woman alive who would drag in King Canute at a moment like this."

"He's very appropriate. Alas."

"Don't say 'alas.' " His face had sobered. "It's been such hell, being around you, wanting you . . . It reminded me a little of when we first met, only this was so much worse." He moved closer, put an arm across her and buried his face between her breasts. "Wanting and wanting and not having," he said, his lips moving on her bare flesh as he spoke. Then, deeply, fiercely,

"Wanting what was mine." He rubbed his cheek against her and she protested a little as the roughness of his beard scratched her tender flesh. He rested his head on her breast and she gently ran her fingers through his touseled black hair.

"It's not like this with anyone else," he said.

"I'm afraid I can't return the compliment," she replied a little acidly. "I haven't got your standard of comparison."

He chuckled. "Thank God for that."

Her fingers continued to move caressingly through his hair. "You'd better go," she said. "I don't want anyone to see you leaving here."

"Why not? We're married."

"Yes—I know." Her fingers stilled and he raised his head to look at her. His nostrils looked suddenly tense.

"I thought you were coming back to me."

"I . . ." She looked up into his face. It was hopeless, she thought. She was weak with love for him. "I suppose I am," she said helplessly.

His face relaxed and the eyes that looked down at her were so dark, so unbearably beautiful. "Then I don't give a damn who sees me," he said and began to kiss her again. He didn't leave for another hour.

She lectured that morning on Hamlet, and as she talked about the problems of the play and the characters she kept seeing Kit's face. What had he meant, she wondered, when he had said that to play Hamlet well he would have to reveal himself?

She did not want anyone at school to know they

had gotten back together again. "Please, Kit," she had said just before he left her that morning. "I need a little time to adjust myself. I can't bear the thought of all these people looking at me the way they will look if they know." Color had stained her cheeks and her voice had trailed off.

He had frowned. "If it was up to me, I'd simply move right in here. There isn't any need for explanations. We're married."

"I know. But I'm not ready yet. Please, Kit," she had said again, this time a little desperately, and he had given in.

She didn't quite know herself why she was so reluctant to make public the fact of their reconciliation. It had something to do with the fact that she was hardly reconciled to the reconciliation herself.

She knew how she felt about him, but she didn't quite trust his feeling for her. He wanted her and he was very adept at getting what he wanted. But would he continue to want her or would it be, as it had been before, a case of out of sight out of mind.

She would have to move to California; she had reluctantly come to that conclusion. He might do an occasional stage play, but the bulk of his work was in the movies and the movie industry was in California. She wanted to be separated from him as little as possible; she remembered all too vividly what had happened the last time they were separated.

She should see a doctor about birth control; that thought crossed her mind a few times during the week that followed. If they kept on the way they were going, she was sure to get pregnant. She would love to have Kit's baby, but she wasn't sure what his reaction would be. She was afraid to ask him. That topic by unspoken consent was taboo between them.

She should send in her resignation to the university as well, but she procrastinated about that too. She felt as if her whole life were off balance and a little unreal; the only reality was the night, when her bedroom door opened and Kit came in.

"It's the strangest feeling, hearing people talk about Chris Douglas," she said to him as the dawn came up on Saturday morning. "I keep thinking, That's *Kit* they're talking about, my husband, the man who neglects to shave before he comes to bed and scratches me all up with his beard."

He gave a warm, sleepy chuckle. "Poor love. I'll shave tomorrow night."

She kissed the top of his head where it lay pillowed on her breast and then went back to her original thought. "I just can't seem to reconcile *that* person, Movie Star Christopher Douglas, with you. It's very peculiar."

"No, it's not," he answered. "Everyone else sees the façade, the reputation, the good nose and the straight teeth. You see *me*. You always have. That's what I love about you. You see right through to the heart of people. Phoniness and sham simply collapse in front of you."

She was silent for a long time. "I think that's one of the nicest things anyone has ever said to me," she said at last.

"Um." She felt his eyelashes against her skin as his eyes closed. Outside the birds began to sing.

"It's getting late," she said. "I hear the birds."

" 'It is not yet near day,' " he answered sleepily. " 'It was the nightingale, and not the lark, that pierced the fearful hollow of thine ear.' "

"Kit!" She laughed and shook him a little. "Stop quoting *Romeo and Juliet* and get up."

"No," he answered simply.

" 'It was the lark, the herald of the morn; no nightingale,' " she quoted back severely.

"You're a spoilsport." He sat up, yawned and stretched. "For how much longer do you mean to keep me creeping in and out of your bedroom in the dead of night? I'm getting too old for such exploits." He got out of bed and picked his jeans up from the bedside chair.

"Until after the play opens," she answered, pushing her hair off her forehead. "I know you think it's silly of me. *I* even think it's silly of me. But I can't help it."

"For a smart woman you can be awfully illogical." He pulled a shirt over his head.

"I know," she replied a little glumly.

"Look, Mary." He sat for a minute on the edge of the bed. "You and I have got to talk. It's no good thinking we can talk at night; I've got other things on my mind when I come in here."

"I'm a little distracted myself," she murmured.

He grinned and kissed the tip of her nose. "Let's go out somewhere for dinner tonight."

"Kit, I would love that," Mary replied fervently. The endless bridge game had gotten on her nerves this last week, but she hadn't known how to get out of it.

"Great. I'll find some quiet spot and make a reservation. Not, I hasten to add, in my own name."

"Will it be all right?" she asked as second thoughts struck her. "What will you tell George?"

"I will tell him that I am taking my wife out to dinner," he said with wicked simplicity, got up off her bed and left.

Chapter Ten

Mary took her time dressing for dinner that evening. She had spent the whole afternoon in the library, hidden away from the press of people she was feeling so acutely this week. It was difficult to behave around Kit as she had last week, when she had been determined to keep him at a distance, and she was afraid her changed feelings were obvious. She felt, with what was perhaps hypersensitivity, that everyone was looking at them, and wondering.

She wore her white linen suit, the dressiest outfit she had brought with her, and took pains with her hair, blowing it dry carefully so it feathered softly back off her face and curled smoothly on her shoulders. At precisely seven o'clock she heard a horn toot outside, and she picked up her black patent leather purse and went out the door.

"How crass," she said as she got into the car. "Honking the horn for me. You might have knocked on my door."

He grinned. "When I was a kid I always longed to pick up my date by blowing on the horn. Unfortunately, I could never afford a car."

"Poor deprived darling," she murmured sympathetically. "Well, if you want to enact your adolescent fantasies, who am I to stop you?"

"Do you want a punch in the nose?" he asked amiably.

She laughed. "Not really. Where are we going?"

"A place George suggested. The Elms, it's called. He said the food is good and the customers are mostly local people."

"Good," said Mary. "You can usually count on New Englanders not to bother you."

It was her first experience of going out with Kit since he had become famous. He parked the car himself in the restaurant lot, and they walked up the stairs of the old clapboard inn and into the lobby. "Mr. Michaels," Kit said pleasantly to the hostess. "I have a reservation for seven-thirty."

The woman's eyes widened as they took him in. She looked nervously at her reservation chart. "Yes, c-certainly," she stuttered. "Come right this way, sir."

Mary was thankful to see it was a corner table, but the walk across the room seemed endless to her. One or two people glanced idly up as they passed and then froze as they recognized Kit's face. It was not a face, Mary thought ruefully as she sat down and regarded him across the table, that one was likely to mistake. He had picked up the menu and for a minute she regarded him, trying to see him as others must, as these people throughout the dining room, all peering surreptitiously at their corner, must see him. She looked and saw a tall, very tan, leanly built man in a lightweight gray suit. His hair was black as coal, black as night, black as hers. He looked up and she smiled a little to herself. She could never see him dispassionately; it was impossible.

"Do you know, I believe this is the first time I've ever seen you in a suit," she said. "It becomes you."

"That's true. I didn't own one when we were married, did I?" The waiter appeared at his elbow and he asked her, "Do you want a drink?"

"Yes. I'll have a vodka martini on the rocks."

"I'll have a whiskey sour," Kit told the waiter.

When the man returned with their drinks he put the martini in front of Kit and the whiskey sour in front of Mary. They exchanged a glance of secret amusement, and after the waiter had gone, Kit changed the drinks. "It's so embarrassing, having a hard drinker for a wife," he said mournfully.

She sipped her martini. "I can't help it if you only like sissy drinks."

"I wasn't brought up in a nice alcoholic middle-class family. I developed a taste for beer at an early age, and I haven't changed."

"You like milk even better," she said.

"Good God, Mary, don't ever let that get out," he said in mock horror. "Think of my rough-and-tough reputation."

She smiled at him, a warm and beautiful smile. "I'll protect your secrets to the death."

"Will you?" He put a hand over hers on the table. Involuntarily she glanced around. At least half the restaurant was looking at him. She pulled her hand away and felt the color flush into her cheeks. "Ignore them," he said. "They're behaving very well, really. After a few minutes they'll stop looking."

She sat back and tried to relax. "I suppose you're used to it by now."

"You never really get used to it. It's just something you have to live with." He glanced over her shoulder. "Ah," he said. "Here it comes."

A man appeared at their table carrying a pad and a pencil. "Mr. Douglas," he said a little nervously and with a definite New York accent. "Would you mind giving me your autograph? It's for my daughter. She just loves your pictures."

As Mary watched, a still and guarded look of cold courtesy settled over Kit's face. It was the mask, she realized, behind which he must have learned to hide from a continual public scrutiny. "I'm sorry," he said coolly, "but I don't give autographs when I am not working."

The man looked nonplussed and backed away a little. "Sorry," he said. Kit nodded coldly and after a minute the man turned and left.

"You were rather brutal," Mary murmured after a minute.

He looked at her. "If I had signed that paper, we'd have had the whole damn restaurant over here for autographs. Now they'll leave us alone."

"Yes," said Mary, a little unhappily. "I suppose that's true."

He smiled at her expression. "You were brought up to be polite. I wasn't. Actually, I don't believe in being polite."

Mary sighed. "I'm learning, believe me."

"Let's order," he said, and handed her the menu.

The meal was delicious and Mary felt herself relaxing as they ate and drank the bottle of wine Kit had ordered to go with it.

"I've decided I'll move to California with you," she said as she savored a perfect filet mignon.

His face blazed into happiness. "Do you mean that?"

"Yes. I can probably work at the UCLA library without any trouble. I don't know about teaching, though. I'd better keep flexible so I can adjust to your schedule."

"Listen to me, Mary." He was deadly earnest. "I want you to have your own life. I do not want you to sacrifice what you want to do for me. If you want to teach, teach. It's what you're trained for."

"Actually, I wasn't," she returned slowly. "I was trained for scholarship. Scholars usually teach so they can eat, not necessarily because they like it."

His eyes were looking deeply into hers. "Did *you* like it?"

Her lips curled a little at the corners. "Not particularly," she said.

His eyes smiled back. "Money isn't a problem, sweetheart. We have plenty of that. If you want to write books, you go right ahead. You don't have to worry about a roof over your head. You can have a housekeeper—a cook—a secretary—whatever you want."

Mary blinked. "Goodness. Do you have all those people?"

"No. I have housekeeper who is extremely crabby but a good cook. We'll have to find another house, though. You'd hate the one I have now."

"Why?"

"It's ghastly," he said cheerfully. "I bought it from some starlet—bought it furnished. I kind of just close my eyes to the inside of it. I took it because it was isolated and I liked the view."

"But why didn't you redo it?" she asked wonderingly.

"I don't know. It didn't seem as if it was worth the effort."

"How long have you had it?"

"Three years."

"Three years!" She stared at him in astonishment. "You've lived in a house you hate for three years and haven't tried to change it?"

He grinned a little lopsidedly. "It was just a place to hang my clothes and park my car. It never felt like a home. No place feels like a home if you're not there."

"Oh, Kit." The words were barely a whisper. She put down her fork and looked at him. "I'll make a home for you, darling."

"I'd like that," he said simply. "Are you sure you don't mind giving up your university job? Won't you miss the contact with all those famous academics?"

"I don't think so," she replied thoughtfully. "I think I might do better at a younger, less venerable institution. All the professors at my place are so—stodgy."

"Even Leonard Fergusson?" He sounded incredulous. Leonard Fergusson was the chairman of her department and a world-renowned scholar.

"I think he's getting old," she replied frankly. "He suffers from a certain inflexibility of thought, which sometimes approaches petrification. He also frequently exhibits a disturbing inability to recognize what century he is living in."

He threw back his head and laughed. "How on earth did he ever hire you?" he asked when he had got his breath back.

"The English department didn't have enough women. They have only *one* tenured female professor, can you believe it? I was to be his second token woman."

"Well, one thing California isn't is stodgy," he said cheerfully. He put down his knife and fork and looked with satisfaction at his empty plate. "That was good."

Mary was only halfway through her steak. "Tell me about California," she said.

"It can be lovely," he answered promptly. "I think this time I'd like to look for a house on the ocean. Would you like that?"

"I'd love it," she answered.

"Maybe I'll get a boat. Like your father's."

Her lips curved tenderly. "That would be fun."

"Yes, it would be. It could be a very decent life, Mary. Not everyone in California is a flake, or a drug addict, you know. Or a movie star."

"Contrary to what my mother thinks," she murmured, and he laughed. "But would we have any privacy, Kit?" All through dinner she had been aware of the watching eyes that surrounded them.

"Money can buy an awful lot," he said a little bitterly. "It can even buy privacy."

"I suppose so," she replied dubiously.

Coffee was served. As she drank it she tried once again to ignore the pressure of watching eyes.

"Have you finished?" Kit asked.

"Yes," she said. They rose and walked back across the restaurant floor—through the battery of staring eyes.

She watched him as he drove back toward campus, watched his long-fingered, sensitive hands as they competently held the wheel, watched his profile, watched his mouth. There is a curious combination of ruthlessness and vulnerability about that mouth, she thought. "What do you think of Margot Chandler?" she asked curiously.

He smiled a little in the darkness of the car. "She's not a bad sort, really. I've met worse."

"What does that mean?"

"It means that she's basically a decent person, that she means no harm to anyone, and that she has an affectionate heart."

"Oh," said Mary rather blankly.

He glanced at her sideways. "What do you think of her?"

"I don't know," she answered carefully. "Her surface is so bright and hard that I haven't been able to get through anywhere. She's the most sophisticated person I've ever met."

"Sophisticated," he said thoughtfully. "Yes, I suppose that is a good way to describe her."

"What word would you use?" she asked, looking at him closely.

"Worldly," he answered promptly. "Like so many Hollywood people, she believes that good can come out of evil, that lies might be better than truth, that the end justifies the means."

"Good God," Mary said faintly. "I thought you said she was basically decent."

"She is—basically. But she's been corrupted. The world does that to people—and the Hollywood world more than most, I suppose."

"You sound very cynical."

They had reached the college gates by now and he swung in, accelerating smoothly up the long drive. "I'm not, really." They came to a halt in front of his cottage. It was about ten-thirty. "How about a walk?" he asked.

"That sounds marvelous," she returned. They had always loved to walk together, and being carless, they had done a lot of it in their early married life. "Let me change my clothes first," she said.

When she came back out of her cottage in sneakers and jeans, she found he was before her, similarly attired. "I found a nice path up through the woods the other morning," he said. "It's too dark to take it now, but I'll show it to you sometime."

She shook her head at him. "You missed your calling, Kit. In some other age you would have been an explorer."

"I would have loved that," he said as he took her hand. "Do you know, I was thinking of doing a movie about David Livingston?" They began to walk down the road together.

"Livingston," she said slowly, on a note of surprise. She thought for a minute. "He was quite a complicated character. Was he a saint or an egomaniac? Or a combination of the two?"

"I should think a good movie would show him as a little of both."

"Yes. Do you have a script?"

"Not yet. I've been thinking of setting up my own

production company. I'd have to borrow some money. There's no way I'm going to touch all my nice safe little investments. But I have a few million free to play around with."

"A few million." She laughed. "I can't quite take it in, Kit. When I think of all the hamburger we used to eat!"

"I know." He put his hand, which was still holding hers, into the pocket of his windbreaker. "But they were the happiest days of my life—those hamburger days."

"Yes," she said. "Mine too."

The sound of music drifted to them. It was coming from the direction of the rec room. They could hear a chorus of lusty young voices raised in song.

"Do you want to go over there?" she asked.

"No." He grimaced a little. "I thought perhaps the college atmosphere here would make me feel like a student again. Instead it's made me feel a million years old."

She laughed. "You aren't exactly a geriatric case, darling, but I know what you mean."

They walked down to the lake and sat for a while in the empty lawn chairs, looking out at the still water. Then they walked back toward the cottages, sometimes talking, sometimes silent, their steps, from long practice, in perfect unison. The students were still singing in the rec room when Mary and Kit walked together into her cottage and went to bed.

Mary woke as the first gray light of dawn was filling the room. She looked at Kit, sleeping peacefully beside her in the double bed. It frightened her a little, what the sight of him did to her. When she was near him she was no longer Dr. O'Connor, the cool, clear-thinking, intelligent, dispassionate scholar. That persona, so carefully built up and nurtured for the last four years, crumbled like straw at the touch of his hand.

She had burned her last bridge last night when she told him she would go to California with him. All that was left now was to send in her resignation. The university would have no problem replacing her; half the academic world would give their right arms for the chance to teach there. And Leonard Fergusson would have confirmed all his prejudices about the untrustworthiness of women teachers.

Why was she so reluctant to write that letter? For she was, and in the gray morning light she realized that she still wasn't completely easy about her decision to go back to Kit. She adored him, but she didn't quite trust him and she hadn't quite forgiven him either. They never spoke about the baby and she knew that until they did, until they laid that sad little ghost to rest, that their marriage would never rest on solid ground. Yet for the life of her she could not bring the subject up. The wound had almost healed, but the scar still ached.

"Good morning," said a deep sleepy voice in her ear.

She turned her head and smiled at him. The smile was a little painful but he didn't seem to notice. "One of the things I've missed most is the way you warm up the bed," she said after a minute. "It's chilly sleeping alone."

"If it's up to me, you'll never sleep alone again," he answered.

She sighed a little and snuggled down under the covers next to him. "That was a melancholy sound," he murmured, and putting his arms around her, he pulled her close. She rested her head against his shoulder and put an arm around him in return. The muscles of his back felt hard and strong under her hand. They were neither of them wearing any clothes.

"This is not a position that is conducive to rest," he murmured after a minute.

"No? I'm comfortable." She closed her eyes.

"Are you, sweetheart?" His hand began to move slowly up and down her back, curving down now and then to caress her hip. She felt a throb deep within her.

"Don't do that," she said.

"All right," he answered softly. "How about this?" He knew exactly where to touch her, exactly how to arouse her. But for some inexplicable reason she did not want to make love now. She pulled away from him a little, but that only gave him room to bend his head and begin to kiss her breasts.

She lay perfectly still as he caressed her body, willing herself to stay separate and apart from him, trying to ignore the rising tumult of her senses. She did not want to give him what he wanted from her; this time at least she would make him take it. She had already given him too much.

"Mary . . ." His shoulders over her blotted out the rest of the room. "Love me," he whispered. She looked up into his eyes, black and glittering; his face was hard with desire. The angry core of separateness within her began to dissolve under his look. They stayed poised like that for a long minute, their eyes locked together. "Love me," he said again. And very very slowly she opened her legs.

As the power and the wonder of him came into her she closed her eyes. It was impossible to deny him, to deny herself; and she arched up against him, lost as always in the flooding majesty of his love. Passion flamed through her blood and thought receded as together they scaled the heights and came, shudderingly, to rest together.

He lay for a long time afterward with his arms locked tightly about her, as if he felt her slipping away and he would hold her to him, by force if necessary.

"It's getting late," she said at last.

"All right." He let her go and rolled over on his back. "For how long are we going to go on playing this game, Mary?"

She put her arm across her eyes to block out his darkly impatient face. "Let me tell my parents before we do anything public," she said.

"Will you call them today?"

"All right." She took her hand away and watched him dress. She felt suddenly ashamed of herself. After all, as he kept pointing out so reasonably, they *were* married. She was behaving like an idiot. She slipped out of bed, pulled her white terry-cloth robe around her and belted it. "Poor darling," she said. "I know I've been unreasonable. I'll call them today, I promise." She put her arm through his and walked with him to the door.

"I may sound like a terrible male chauvinist, but it bothers the hell out of me to see you with other men and not be able to show myself as the 'man in possession.'"

"That does sound terribly like a male chauvinist," she said softly. "But I love you anyway." He had opened the porch door and was standing framed in the doorway. She reached up on tiptoe to kiss him. His arms came around her.

There was a flash of light and then another one. Mary felt Kit's body stiffen and then he pushed her away from him. She stared in numbed astonishment. Out on the road in front of them was Jason Razzia, with his camera.

Kit cursed under his breath, a word she had never heard him use before. His eyes were wild with anger, and with the swiftness of a panther he was down the porch steps and running toward the photographer.

Jason Razzia backed up toward the woods as he saw Kit coming. Then he turned to run, but he wasn't quick enough. A lean, hard hand shot out and grabbed him by the shoulder. The other hand pulled the camera from him and sent it smashing down against a rock.

"Hey!" said Razzia. "You can't do that."

"I just did it," said Kit. "And I'll smash your head in the same way if you don't clear out of here." His searing anger had such force that for the first time since childhood Razzia found himself physically afraid of another person. He tried to pull away from Kit's iron grip.

"I'm g-going," he stuttered. Murder was looking at him out of Kit's dark eyes.

"And stay away from my wife," said Kit between his teeth. His voice was low and absolutely menacing. "If I catch you anywhere around her, I'll kill you. Do you hear me?"

"Yeah, Chris. Yeah, I hear you. Sorry. I'm going . . ." Razzia was shaking now and Kit shoved him toward the woods.

"Get out of here, you scum." Razzia ran.

Slowly, very slowly, Kit swung around and looked at his wife. She was still in the doorway of the porch and he could see from where he was standing that she was shivering. He cursed again, silently, bent to pick up the shattered camera, and then walked back to where she stood. Instinctively, she backed away from him. He stopped. "It had to happen in front of you," he said. Anyone who did not know him would not have heard the fierce anger that lay under the flat tone. "Any other woman in the world would have gotten a cheap thrill out of that. But not you."

Mary's eyes were dark in her white face. Her hands were clutched, protectively, on the front of her robe, holding it together. Kit had himself under control now, but he still wore the menacing aspect a male assumes when he is really angry. She was afraid of him.

"Let's go inside," he said in a calmer voice.

"No." She backed up onto the porch. "No, It's no good, Kit. I couldn't stand it. Photographers snooping around, peeking in my bedroom window. It's horrible!"

He followed her into the porch. "You don't mean that. One little incident like this can't make any difference between you and me."

"It does," she replied shakily.

His hand grasped her shoulder and she winced at the pressure of his fingers. "You only say that because you're upset."

"I am upset," she said. "But I mean it. I can't go back to you, Kit. I can't."

He let her go. His mouth looked taut and thin. "I'm not going to beg you, Mary." His voice was deeply bitter.

"I don't want you to."

"If this is your final decision, I'll abide by it."

"Oh, God, Kit," she cried. "Will you please just *go?*"

He dropped his hand from her shoulder, turned and walked out the door. She went inside and collapsed in a shivering heap on the sofa.

After a long time she got up and went in to shower. It was Sunday, she realized in stunned surprise. She would have to go to Mass.

She dried her hair, put on a print summer-dress, and walked out to her car. She felt numb. It was a state that continued all through the first part of the Mass, as she automatically made the responses, standing and sitting and kneeling like an automaton.

When she came back from communion, she knelt and bowed her face between her hands. It was quiet in the church, with only the organ playing. Dear God, she prayed, help me. What have I done?

It isn't true, she thought, eyes closed, shut in on herself, it couldn't be true that she had rejected Kit simply because a photographer had taken their picture. That ugly little scene had been the catalyst, not the cause, of her decision. Nor had she sent Kit away because he had punched out the despicable Razzia. It was something else, she realized.

Communion was over and the congregation stood for the final blessing. As the rest of the people in the church filed out Mary knelt back down. Once more she bowed her head. Her reaction to Kit this morning, she thought, had its roots deep in the past. She loved him, yes, but there was a dark side to his nature that she had encountered before and it was that aspect of him that she had recoiled from this morning.

He had come into her life five years ago like some splendid young god, sweeping her off her balance, out of her safe, familiar setting and into the passionate, ecstatic world of sexual love. But she had found, as had so many unfortunate Greek maidens before her, that it is dangerous to love a god. Gods, as classical literature should have taught her, tend to look out primarily for their own self-interest.

Kit had looked out for his, and at her expense. Contrary to what he claimed, he didn't need her. He was the most frighteningly self-sufficient person she had ever known. If something or someone got in his way, he smashed it, as he had smashed that camera this morning.

In the dim quiet of the church she looked up at the statue of the Virgin on the side altar. She was holding the infant Christ in her arms. Looking at that serene image of motherhood, Mary recognized that she had never forgiven Kit for suggesting an abortion to her. When the baby had died she had felt that he had almost willed it to happen. It still lay between them. It always would. And that was why she had rejected him this morning. Very slowly she rose to her feet and walked out of the church.

She went back to the college and worked on Elizabethan songbooks all afternoon. When she went over to the dining hall for dinner, she devoutly hoped that Kit would not be there. He was. She saw him standing by the fireplace as soon as she walked into the rec room. Tonight he did not turn to look at her.

He didn't sit at her table for dinner either. Mary, seated between George and Alfred Block, was aware in all her nerve endings of his tall dark figure at the table next to hers, but she forced her eyes and her outward attention to George and Alfred and the students who were sitting with her.

After dinner they went back into the rec room and there it was even worse. To the onlooker, she supposed, they were no different than they had been all last week: polite, civilized toward each other, indifferent. But last week they had been playing a game. This was for real.

"We missed you at dinner last night, Chris," Mary heard Carolyn say to him.

"Mary and I went into town for dinner," he replied coolly. "It made for a change."

They had all known that, of course. The two of them couldn't have been absent together without causing a great deal of speculation. "Are you two getting back together again?" asked Eric Lindquist sunnily.

"As a matter of fact"—and here Kit's eyes met hers—"we were discussing a divorce."

She felt as though someone had hit her over the head with a brick. His eyes were coal-black and inimical. She put her hand up to brush a nonexistent strand of hair off her cheek. Everyone was staring at her. "I suppose it's time we did something about this unorthodox situation," she said. She went to pick up her coffee cup and discovered her hand was shaking. She hastily put it down again. "How about some bridge?" she asked Melvin Shaw. She managed to play for two hours without remembering a single card she had in her hand.

Chapter Eleven

The play was due to open the following Saturday night and for the remainder of the week George worked his cast hard. It was the only thing in the whole dreadful week that Mary had cause to be grateful for. Kit spent almost all his waking hours in the theater and Mary was spared the achingly painful sight of him for most of the day. He skipped dinner a few nights as well; the same nights that Margot was absent. She supposed, Mary thought dully, that she should be grateful for that as well.

The result of the heavy rehearsal schedule was that Mary had too much time alone. Ordinarily she would have relished the opportunity for solitude in such lovely surroundings, but in her present emotional state she needed the distraction of other people. When she was by herself, she tended to think of Kit. It didn't do any good to think of Kit, she didn't want to think of Kit, but she did think of Kit. Continually. She took to spending her afternoons in the library working on the

Elizabethan songbooks. If it was not the vacation she had envisioned, at least it was better than continually brooding about what could not be helped.

On Thursday she slipped into the dark of the theater and sat down in a chair in the back row. It was the first time she had ever come to a rehearsal. She hadn't meant to come today, but the pull had been too strong. She didn't think anyone had noticed her entrance.

Kit was halfway through the third soliloquy. Carolyn Nash, as Ophelia, was at stage right, kneeling in silent prayer, her back to Kit. Mary thought the scene looked rather awkward, and George apparently had come to the same conclusion. She heard his voice calling, "Hold up a minute, Chris!" He got up from his chair in the front row and went to the edge of the stage. In a minute he had jumped up, and Mary watched as he rearranged Carolyn so that she was turned more toward the audience. He was saying something to her, but Mary could not hear him. He walked back to the edge of the stage and jumped down. "Let's try it again," he said. Kit walked off the stage. "All right," George called. "Now."

Very slowly Kit came back on, his head bowed, his eyes on the ground. The scene looked very strange to Mary. Both Kit and Carolyn were wearing jeans and sneakers. In a low yet perfectly audible voice Kit began. "To be, or not to be, that is the question."

Mary listened carefully, all her senses trained on the man on stage. His voice is like no other actor's, she thought. The voice alone would get him through. He looked up and saw Ophelia. Mary sat forward on

the edge of her chair. She was curious as to how
George would stage the "nunnery" scene.

It was not as physical as many she had seen. It was,
if anything, restrained. George stopped it once to say
to Kit, "*You've* got to generate the intensity of this
scene, Chris. It would be easy for me to let you toss
Carolyn around and throw the furniture, but I'm not
going to do that. For one thing, I don't want Carolyn
all bruised up."

"Thank you, George," the girl put in with a grin.

He smiled back at her. "And more importantly, I
want to establish the feeling that Hamlet is *holding in*.
He's a keg of dynamite about to explode. He doesn't
explode—yet. But you've got to give out vibes, Chris.
You've got to be scary."

Kit had been listening courteously. Now he nodded.
"Yes. I see."

"All right. Let's take the scene from where you
look up and see her."

They began again. Someone came over in the dark
and sat down next to Mary. "You haven't been in here
before," said the unmistakably English voice of Melvin Shaw.

Mary smiled a little and wished he would go away.
"No."

"What do you think?" he asked her.

"What do *you* think?" she returned. "You've done a
lot of Shakespeare. You've seen how this production is
shaping up."

"I don't know quite what I think," he returned
slowly. "To be frank, I wasn't at all pleased to dis-
cover that Chris had replaced Adrian Saunders. I almost pulled out."

"Why didn't you?"

"I believe in sticking to my contracts, for one thing. And George has acquired a rather good reputation recently. A reputation that is deserved, incidently. He has a great deal of respect for the play as it is written. But any *Hamlet* lives or dies by the actor who plays the lead."

"Oh," said Mary. "Kit sounded good to me," she added cautiously.

"He needs more fire," said Melvin Shaw. "He's got all the equipment to do the part. He's the only American actor I've ever known who has a genuine feel for the language. He's got the intelligence. But does he have the soul?"

"I think he does," she said defensively.

"Well, my dear, Saturday night will tell us." He smiled at her. "I'm looking forward to our bridge game this evening."

Mary's heart sank. "So am I," she answered hollowly.

George began to call for Melvin, and as soon as he had walked down the aisle Mary slipped out of her seat and out the theater door.

She begged out of the bridge game that night. Kit and Margot had been at dinner and she felt she couldn't bear to spend the evening playing cards and listening to Margot play up to Kit. "I have a headache," she said to Melvin with an apologetic smile. "I think I'll have an early evening."

He looked extremely glum. "I'll turn in too, then. Good night, my dear."

She turned and found George beside her. "I'll walk back with you," he said.

"All right." The night was chilly and she put her arms into her sweater as they went up the hill to the cottages.

"What did you think of our rehearsal this afternoon?" he asked.

"I didn't think you saw me," she returned in surprise.

"I have a sixth sense where you're concerned," he said. She didn't reply and after a minute he repeated, "What did you think?"

"I was there for less than half an hour, but from what I saw I thought it looked good. Are you pleased?"

"Pretty much. It's coming together. Alfred has surprised me. He's very strong as Claudius."

"Well that's good," she answered. They had reached her cottage. "Claudius needs to be strong."

He smiled down at her. "Will you invite me in for a drink?"

She hesitated. She hadn't missed George's comment earlier about having a sixth sense where she was concerned, and she didn't want to lead him on. On the other hand, she knew she wouldn't sleep at this early hour and she did not fancy spending the next few hours alone.

"Of course," she said. "Come on in."

She mixed Scotches and went to sit on the sofa. "I thought Carolyn did well this afternoon," she said as soon as he was seated in the wing chair.

"Yes. She has the kind of fragile prettiness one

needs for Ophelia. And she can act. I think she'll be one of those who make it."

Silence fell. Her throat felt dry and she sipped her drink. They were both studiously avoiding talking about the one person they were both thinking about. George brought the subject up first. "I don't know if Chris is going to come through or not."

"How do you mean?" Her voice sounded husky and she took another swallow of her drink.

"There's something missing. He has everything down; he hasn't put a foot wrong on stage all week. But . . ." He frowned a little, trying to find the right words.

"Melvin said he needed more fire."

"It isn't just that, either. The damnable thing is, I feel as if he has it and is holding it back. But I may be wrong."

"Well," she said weakly. "I suppose Saturday night will tell."

"It certainly will. There will be critics from three TV networks, two national magazines, and the *New York Times* in the audience. I usually get the critics sometime during the course of August, but this is shaping up into a regular opening night.

"God have mercy," said Mary.

He grinned. "It's not God's mercy we need, but John Calder's. He's the *Times* theater critic and he's the one who will decide our fate. If he likes it, we'll almost certainly get a Broadway run."

"Broadway," she said. "My goodness."

He put his drink down and came over to sit next to her on the sofa. "I'm tired of talking about the play," he said. "I want to talk about you."

Her blue eyes widened and she looked a little warily into his face. "What do you mean?"

"Is it true that you and Chris are getting a divorce?"

There was a barely perceptible hesitation and then
she said, quite firmly, "Yes."

"I am very glad to hear that." He took her drink
from her unresisting hand. "You are driving me absolutely crazy," he said. And kissed her.

His mouth was warm and hard and insistent on
hers. She was quiet in his arms, letting him kiss her
but giving him very little response.

"Mary," he said shakily and touched her cheek.

"Oh George," she said sadly. "I didn't mean this to
happen."

"I should imagine it must happen to you all the
time." She had been looking at the open collar of his
shirt, but when his words registered she raised her
eyes to his face. At the flash of blue a muscle flickered
alongside his mouth. "I don't mean that you try to be
provocative," he said. "Quite the contrary, as a matter
of fact. But you're quite a special lady. Any man
would want to get near you."

"No one ever has," she replied in a low voice, "except Kit."

"Whom you are going to divorce."

"I—yes."

"I don't want to rush you, Mary, but I should like
so much to be more to you than just a friend."

She looked searchingly into his narrow, clever, attractive face. She liked George very much. She had
thought once she would marry a man very like him. "I
had no idea you felt like this," she said honestly.

"I thought for a while there that you and Chris were going to get back together."

"I thought so too. For a while." She took a deep breath. "I love him, George. I think I always will. But I can't live with him."

He was staring intently at her face. "Why not?"

"Oh—reasons," she replied evasively. "But the thing is, I'm just not interested in anyone else. Not that way, at least. I like you very much, but . . ."

Her voice trailed off and he finished her sentence for her, ". . . as a friend."

"Yes," she said. "I'm sorry it sounds so trite."

"Look here," he said strongly, "I hope you aren't planning to spend the rest of your life alone just because your marriage didn't work out."

"That's what Hamlet advises Ophelia," she replied a little bitterly, " 'What should such fellows as I do, crawling between earth and heaven? We are arrant knaves all; believe none of us. Go thy ways to a nunery.' "

"Don't be an idiot," he snapped. "This is the twentieth century, not the sixteenth. And Ophelia was a simp."

Mary's lips curled at the corners. "She was, rather, wasn't she?"

"Mary," he said, his voice a note deeper than usual. "Beautiful, beautiful Mary. Listen to me. . . ."

"No." She pulled back from him and stared with somber eyes across the room. "No, George. Please don't upset me by saying things I don't want to hear. It isn't just my feelings for Kit. There are religious reasons, too."

"All right." He sounded suddenly very weary. He got to his feet. "But don't run away from me? Will you promise me that at least?"

She smiled a little. "Yes."

He stopped for a minute and held her face between his hands. "I can be a very patient man," he said softly and kissed her forehead before he turned and left the room.

Friday was the last day of class. Technically there was nothing to hold Mary any longer at Yarborough. She could grade her papers at home and telephone the marks to George. After telling herself all week that she couldn't wait to get away, it was distressing to find herself so reluctant when the moment of release finally arrived.

She had to be here on opening night; she had to see for herself how Kit was going to fare. It was as simple as that. When it came right down to it, she thought in grim amusement as she stuffed the final essays into her briefcase, wild horses couldn't drag her away.

She spent all day on her porch, reading essays and grading them. When she went down to dinner it was to find Kit, Margot, Melvin, Alfred, and George missing. They were in the theater going over the scene in Gertrude's bedroom, Carolyn told Mary. George had sent over for sandwiches.

Mary felt the tension in the dining room. It was quieter than usual and the only talk that was introduced had to do with the play. "Poor Chris," said Frank Moore as the main course was served. "I know *I'm* exhausted—we worked on the fencing scene all day long. And he's still going strong. I don't know how he does it."

"And keeps his temper," put in Adam Truro. They ate for a few minutes in silence and then Adam volunteered, "John Calder is going to stay at the Stafford Inn. George says it's the first time a New York critic has ever come for his opening night."

"If the play does go to Broadway," breathed Carolyn, "I wonder if they'll replace all the students?"

"We have to get to Broadway first," said Eric Lindquist. "And we all know who that depends on." He looked in the direction of the theater and the whole table unconsciously followed his lead.

"I wonder what he's thinking," said Frank, and no one asked to whom he was referring.

"He's so calm." Carolyn's eyes were large with wonder. "He must know how his whole professional reputation is at stake, but you'd never know it to look at him. He hasn't any nerves at all."

Oh yes he has, thought Mary to herself. She remembered other opening nights. The calmer Kit appeared the more uptight he really was. She found herself completely unable to eat her dinner.

Saturday was interminable. Even the Elizabethan songbooks couldn't capture Mary's attention. There was an early dinner served at five o'clock. Everyone was present in the dining room and the atmosphere was brittle with tension. Kit was there this time, looking cool and collected. Mary found herself at the same table with him and she listened as he made Carolyn laugh with a joke and flattered Margot outrageously

until some of the strain left her face. He seemed utterly relaxed, utterly nonchalant. Mary wondered if
she were the only one to notice that he had eaten
scarcely a bite of his dinner.

The meal was almost over when Carolyn repeated
the judgment she had voiced about him yesterday.
"Honestly, Chris, I don't think you have a nerve in
your whole body."

"I believe Hemingway called it 'grace under
pressure,' " Mary said quietly. She had scarcely spoken at all during the course of the meal.

Kit's eyes involuntarily found hers. She smiled at
him, a sweet and beautiful smile. "Good luck," she
said softly.

He didn't answer but nodded his dark head at her,
his eyes grave and a little abstracted.

After dinner Mary went back to her cabin to
change. It was six o'clock. The hour and a half before
curtain time stretched before her. She tried to read a
magazine but couldn't concentrate on more than one
sentence at a time.

Finally it was time to dress. She put on a raspberry
linen sundress with a pleated bodice and full skirt. A
string of pearls around her neck dressed it up as did
pearl-button earrings. Her hair fell loosely to her shoulders, satiny black, softly curling. It was cooling down
so she put a white piqué jacket over her bare shoulders. She didn't know if it was the evening air or ner-
vousness, but she was shivering by the time she
reached the theater.

She had a seat in the third row and looked around
her, trying to pick out the critics. The lights were dim-

ming when George slipped into the seat next to hers. "That's Calder there," he murmured in her ear.

Mary stared at the gray head in front of her. "Oh." The lights went out and she closed her eyes, breathing a wordless prayer of supplication. When she opened them the curtain was slowly rising, revealing Dan Palmer and Mark Ellis, two of her students, dressed as soldiers. "Who's there?" said Mark sharply. The play was on.

Mary sat tensely throughout the first scene. George had handled the ghost very skillfully, she thought, using shadows and a tape recorder. The stage was cleared and then, with a fanfare of trumpets, the court swept on.

In center stage, on twin gilt chairs, sat Alfred Block and Margot Chandler—the King and Queen. Surrounding them was a mass of courtiers dressed in bright clothing: Melvin Shaw as Polonius, Frank Moore as Laertes, Carolyn Nash as Ophelia, and various other students. In the corner, apart, wearing severe black, was Kit. Alfred began his speech:

> Though yet of Hamlet our dear brother's death
> The memory be green, and that is us befitted
> To bear our hearts in grief . . .

Alfred's voice was strong, his bearing dominant, but Mary's whole attention was focused on the still, black figure in the corner. Gradually, as the scene went on, she realized that she was not alone in her reaction. The people seated around her were watching

Kit as well. Finally came the line she was waiting for: "But, now, my cousin Hamlet, and my son—" said Alfred.

Kit didn't look up, didn't move, but his whole tense figure seemed to quiver at the words. "A little more than kin, and less than kind!" His beautiful voice was edged with bitterness and scorn. Next to her Mary heard George let out his breath, as though he had been holding it for a long time.

George's confidence seemed to increase as the first act progressed. At the end of it—as Kit said despairingly:

"The time is out of joint, O cursed spite,
    That ever I was born to set it right!"

—George leaned over and whispered to Mary, "He's pulling it off. He didn't have this in rehearsals."

At the first intermission it seemed that the audience agreed with George. Mary wandered around the lobby, assiduously eavesdropping, and general opinion seemed to be that Kit was remarkably good. As Mary heard one lady say to her friend, "My dear, that voice! I think I could listen to him recite the telephone directory and be happy."

The audience settled back in their chairs and the play resumed. It opened with Act III, the "To be or not to be" soliloquy, and the nunnery scene. And it was then that Mary, and the rest of the audience as well, began to realize what it was that they were seeing. Kit seemed to have himself under iron control. His voice was harsh and low; only twice did he forget himself and begin to shout. But the force of emotion he generated was overpowering: the anger, the pain, the furious sense of betrayal, it was all there. You have to be scary, George had told him. He was.

And he was so much more. He reached into the heart of the character and laid bare all the anguish that underlay Hamlet's wild and enigmatic behavior. The blighted ideals, the betrayed love, the aching uncertainty, and above all else, the poignant and unbearable loneliness. His big scene with Margot, the one that George had rehearsed and rehearsed yesterday, was absolutely shattering. When it was over, Mary realized, a little dazedly, that Kit had been right about Margot. She made the perfect Gertrude: lovely, sexual, affectionate, but shallow. The power of the scene came from the contrast between her grief and repentance, which manifested itself in easy tears, and his, which was harsh and violent, tearing apart his heart and his mind.

The intermission that followed this scene was different from the first one. People were quiet now, almost subdued. No one showed a disposition to linger over his cigarette and stillness had fallen over the auditorium even before the lights had begun to dim for the opening of Act IV.

The last two acts were stunning in their emotional impact. What moved Mary more than anything else was the way she could see aspects of Kit's real character coming through the words and emotions of Hamlet. When he leaped into Ophelia's grave after Laertes, his bitter searing anger reminded her vividly of the morning he had gone after Jason Razzia.

The final dueling scene with Frank Moore had the audience on the edge of their seats. "Frank fenced on his college team," George murmured in Mary's ear. "That was one of the reasons I chose him for Laertes."

Kit's fencing was a match for Frank's. He must have put in long hours of practice, thought Mary, as she watched the swords flashing on stage. The final moment had almost arrived: the infuriated Laertes, unable to break through Hamlet's guard, stabbed his unsuspecting opponent between bouts with his sharp and poisoned sword. There was a moment of breathless silence as Kit looked down at his wounded arm and realized for the first time that Laertes was playing with a sharp sword. His eyes narrowed, his breath hissed between his teeth, and he advanced on Laertes, sword up.

The two men began to fight again, not in a sporting contest this time, but for blood. The clash of swords and the heaviness of their breathing were the only sounds in the entire theater. Finally Kit, with a strong skillful stroke, struck the sword from Laertes hand. Bending, he picked it up. Slowly he held out to Laertes his own sword, which was blunt and harmless. His face was implacable, and Laertes, knowing as he did that the sword Kit retained was not only sharp but also tipped with deadly poison, was forced to accept. The fight resumed.

Mary's hands were clasped tensely in her lap. She knew what would happen, even knew the exact words that would be spoken, but when they came, when Kit cried out in a terrible voice of mingled anguish and fury;

"O villainy! Ho! let the door be locked.
Treachery! Seek it out,"

she felt her hand go, involuntarily, to her throat.

It stayed there throughout the remainder of the scene, as Adam Truro, playing Horatio, clasped the dying Hamlet in his arms. His broken voice uttering the famous farewell, "Good night, sweet prince, and flights of angels sing thee to thy rest!" brought stinging tears to her eyes.

There was the sound of drums and Eric Lindquist, blond, handsome, boyish Eric, playing Fortinbras, came marching in. His clear blue eyes swept around the stage, littered with the corpses of Laertes, Gertrude, Claudius, and Hamlet. He reared his golden head: "I have some rights of memory in this kingdom," he said clearly, "which now to claim my vantage doth invite me."

The contrast was devastating: the brilliant, tortured, complex Hamlet and this sunshiny boy who saw in the cataclysmic ruin before him only his own advantage.

The muffled drums began to roll and four students stepped forward to lift Kit's still body up, high in the air above their heads. Eric's voice rolled out across the audience, over the drums:

Let four captains
Bear Hamlet like a soldier to the stage,
For he was likely, had he been put on,
To have proved most royal; and for his passage

The soldiers' music and the rite of war
Speak loudly for him.

The soldiers carrying Kit moved slowly up the scaffolding that represented the castle steps. In the distance a gun began to shoot. They reached the top of
the scaffolding and stood still, Kit's body still raised
high above them. The curtain fell.

For fully half a minute there was not a sound in the
theater. Then the clapping began, at first a ripple,
then a growing tide as the curtain calls began.
Tremendous applause greeted the supporting cast,
with Margot getting the biggest hand of all. Then, out
on to the stage to join his fellow performers, came
Kit. The theater erupted in a storm of acclaim. He
smiled, bowed, and held out his hands to Margot and
Carolyn. The curtain came down but the clapping refused to subside. At last it came up again to reveal
Kit, alone on the stage. The audience rose to its feet
in thunderous ovation. Mary felt herself crying. It was
the most overwhelming tribute she had ever heard an
audience bestow on a performer. She turned to look at
George. His face was glowing. "You did it." He
seemed to be talking to Kit across the avalanche of
sound. "I wasn't sure if you would, but by Christ you
pulled it out. Best goddamn Hamlet I ever saw."

Mary picked up her purse to fish for a tissue. "And
you directed it," she said shakily.

"No." He shook his head and looked at her. "No
one directed what Chris did tonight. That he did all
by himself." He grinned. "The SOB was saving it up.
And I was scared to death. Wait until I get my hands
on him." The crowd was beginning to move toward

the exits. "I'm going backstage," said George to Mary. "Coming?"

"Not just yet," she replied. "You go ahead." As he walked toward the front of the theater she took her place in the crowd that was leaving by the rear exit.

Chapter Twelve

✦

She went back to her cottage and sat down in the living room. She understood now what Kit meant when he had said that to do Hamlet well he would have to reveal himself. In order to portray the emotions he had this evening he had first to have felt them. And then he had to show what he had felt up there on the stage.

Kit was a very private person. His strong feelings about his privacy had always been a source of despair to his agent and to the various publicity people who had been associated with his pictures. Mary understood that part of him, that passionate feeling of not wanting to be exposed, written about, journalized. For such a man to do what he had done tonight—the sheer blazing courage it had taken to get up on a stage and reveal all *that*—shook her profoundly.

She felt that for the first time since she had known him she was seeing him as he really was. She had never associated him with any weakness. He was so splendidly male, so tough and strong, such a dominant lover; he had seemed invulnerable to her. But tonight she had seen something else. She had seen a man who knew what it was to love, to be rejected, to be betrayed, and above all, to be alone.

For the first time she considered the possibility that she had failed him more deeply than he had failed her. She had never given him a chance. She had driven him away, and in so doing she had hurt him badly. She had seen that tonight, in the scene with Ophelia.

She thought of all that she had seen tonight and she felt humbled and ashamed and cowardly. She had been so afraid of being hurt herself that she had taken no thought for the hurt she might be inflicting. And she claimed she loved him. Poor Kit, she thought. He deserved better. He had told her once that she saw through to the heart of him, but that wasn't true. If she had, she would not have sent him away without giving him a chance to explain.

He would be tied up with the cast party for a while, but she didn't want to see him in a crowd of people. And she wanted to see him tonight—she felt she must see him tonight. She left her cottage and walked resolutely next door to his, went in and curled up on the sofa, prepared to wait.

He came about an hour later. There was a frown on his face as he pushed the door open; the light had warned him someone was waiting for him. "It's only me," she said quietly from the sofa.

"Mary!" He sounded surprised and a wary look came over his face. "What are you doing here?" He came into the room and dropped rather heavily into the wing chair. She noted with a pang of anxiety that he looked very tired.

Now that she faced him she didn't quite know what to say. He looked so weary. She said with a curious note of huskiness and uncertainty in her voice, "I only came to tell you that if you still want me back, I'll come. But if you tell me to get out, I certainly won't blame you."

He closed his eyes. All the muscles in his face went rigid. When he opened them again he said, "Do you mean it this time? I don't think I can take it if you change your mind again."

Tears began to pour down her face. "Oh, darling, I'm so sorry. I've been so horrible. And I love you so much. Please, please take me back." She wasn't sure who made the first move, but three seconds later she was in his lap, locked in his arms, her head buried in his shoulder. She continued to cry. "I've been so afraid of you, afraid of loving you," she got out. "You hurt me so much before."

"I know I did," he replied. His own voice was husky with emotion. "Mary"—his arms tightened, his lips were in her hair—"I was so sorry about the baby, sweetheart, I was so sorry."

Her body was shaking with sobs but she made no attempt to stop them. She felt as if a hard knot that had been lodged within her for four years was slowly dissolving and washing away with her tears. "I blamed you," she said into his shoulder.

"I know," he repeated. "I knew, as soon as I got that call from your mother, that I had made the biggest mistake of my life in neglecting you. All the way in on the plane, I knew it in my bones."

"But why, Kit? Why didn't you ever call me? Why did you just—disappear?"

"It was unforgivable. I know that now—I knew it as soon as I got your mother's call. But I was like a man driven, Mary. I pushed everything that wasn't my career to the back of my mind—and that included you. I knew this was my only chance to make it and I just grabbed everything that could possibly be useful. Even Jessica Corbet. I didn't go to bed with her, but I didn't try to squash those rumors either. I think I must have been a little mad."

"Your only chance?" Her sobs were lessening now and she lifted her head to look at him. "What do you mean?"

"I mean that if I hadn't made it with *The Russian Experiment*—if I hadn't gotten another picture with a good salary out of it—I was going to quit acting."

Her eyes were great blue pools of astonishment. "Quit acting! But why?"

"Because I was going to be a father and I was damned if I'd have my kid raised the way I was. I had to give him financial security. And I was damned if I was going to let you stop your studies because we couldn't afford a baby-sitter. I have a math degree—I was going to see if I couldn't get a job in computers."

"Computers!" She couldn't have looked more horrified if he had said he was going to run numbers. He smiled a little at her expression. "But why didn't you tell me?"

"Because of the way you look now," he replied. "And I thought that if I put everything I had into it, that I *would* make good in Hollywood. And I did. But in the process I lost everything that mattered." He put his cheek against her hair and held her to him. "I lost my son. And I lost you." There was a long moment of silence, then he said, as if he found the words difficult, "Where did you bury him?"

She felt a fierce pain about her heart at what she had shut him out from. "In St. Thomas's, next to my grandparents. I'll take you there if you like."

"Yes," he said very low. "I'd like that."

She closed her eyes. "I was such a beast," she whispered.

"No, you weren't. You weren't in any state to listen to explanations. I realized that and that's why I did what you asked and left. After I thought you had had a chance to recover a little, I wrote you. I wrote you twice, telling you just what I've told you tonight. But you never answered."

"I tore the letters up."

"I see." His voice was flat.

"I told you I blamed you." She took her head out of his shoulder and spoke somberly. "If there's one thing the Irish know how to do, Kit, it's nurse a grudge. I'm really not a very nice person. I don't know why you even want me back."

He smiled at her and there was pain as well as tenderness in his look. "No, you're not 'nice.' You are intelligence and integrity, beauty and passion. It's like touching solid ground in a quagmire to touch you again."

She cupped his face between her hands. "I never really thought you needed me," she said. "Not like I needed you."

"You seem to have gotten along fine without me,"

he returned. His face was very still between her palms. "You have your job, your family."

She kissed him. "I was operating on half a heart." She kissed him again and felt him begin to smile.

"I know. All these years I've felt as if something of me was left out. It's only when I'm with you that I feel that I'm a whole person again."

She sighed and snuggled, if possible, even closer. "To think we owe all this to that wretched magazine," she murmured.

"What magazine, sweetheart?"

"The one that found out we were married and spread my picture all over the front page. If it hadn't been for that, you would never have come to see me. And I would never have told you I was working at Yarborough."

"True," he sounded a little cautious.

"You did come to Yarborough because you knew I'd be here, didn't you?"

"Yes."

"I thought the whole setup was too neat to be a coincidence," she said complacently.

"Actually, I called my agent right after I saw you." He was speaking slowly, carefully, as if testing her reaction: "I told him just to get me in, I'd play any part. It was only luck that Adrian Saunders got that movie offer. Otherwise I might have been stealing one of the student's parts."

She sat back on his lap and stared at him. "Good heavens, I'd no idea you'd done that. I thought that when the part became available you'd taken it because you knew I would be here."

"No." He looked measuringly into her eyes and

seemed to be reassured by what he saw there. "I have another confession to make."

She compressed her lips a little. "What is it?"

"I was the one who leaked the story of our marriage to *Personality*."

"You what!" Her eyes were wide with incredulity.

"I leaked the story," he repeated. "I was desperate to see you again and I couldn't think of any reason for me to present myself. And then, too, I thought that making the marriage public would force you to do something about it. You hadn't even tried to get a legal separation, so I hoped that maybe there was a chance you'd consider coming back to me."

"You stinker," she said, but the lines of her mouth were soft.

He grinned. "It worked."

"Why couldn't you just have come to see me?"

"Would you have listened to me if I'd arrived at your doorstep, hat in hand?" He looked at her skeptically.

Her lips curled a little. "No, I suppose not. I was too well armored in all my grudges."

"Well, the course I took was crude, I'll admit that. But it was effective." He smoothed her hair back from her forehead. "Do you know something?" he asked in a kind of astonishment. "I'm starving."

"Of course you are," she answered sympathetically. "You didn't eat a bite of your dinner." She pushed herself off his lap and stood up. "I have some peanut butter and jelly in my fridge. Come on and I'll make you a sandwich."

He stood up and staggered a little. "Ow! I think you cut off all the circulation in my legs."

"You're so romantic," she murmured. He hobbled around the room for a bit and she watched him, smiling. When he finally came to a halt she said, "Bring your toothbrush and pajamas and a change of clothes."

He swung around with no suggestion of stiffness at all. "What did you say?"

"You heard me," she returned serenely. "I won't even push you out in the morning."

He heaved a great dramatic sigh. "Thank God for that. I've come to the conclusion that I'm really a very domestic type. All this creeping about in the dead of night doesn't appeal to me at all."

It was true, she thought, as she watched him collect his things. He looked like every woman's dream lover, but he had been happy as a clam refinishing furniture and painting walls in their first apartment. And he had not been indifferent to the thought of fatherhood; quite the contrary. If he had been willing to give up acting for it, he took it very seriously indeed.

She thought back to that dreadful argument they had had when she first told him she was pregnant. She remembered how angry he had been when she said she would give up her fellowship. It had upset her dreadfully, that anger. She had not realized that it sprang from his great and generous love, from his passionate desire to see her free to fulfill the promise that was in her. He still felt the same way. She remembered how concerned he had been when she had said she would give up teaching.

They walked together in companionable silence back to her cottage. He sat down and stretched his long legs in front of him while she made the sandwiches and poured two glasses of apple juice. He looked at her in admiration as he bit into the peanut-butter-and-jelly sandwich.

"You're wonderful," he said. "You always have whatever's needed right on hand."

She laughed at him. "Just like the mother in *The Swiss Family Robinson*."

"Well," he replied dryly, "not quite."

He finished his sandwich and yawned. Mary did the same. "I'm dead," she said. "You use the bathroom first and I'll clean up these crumbs." In five minutes they were both in pajamas and in bed. In seven minutes they were asleep.

Mary woke to find the sun streaming into the bedroom. She had been so tired last night that she hadn't closed the shade. She hopped out of bed, drew the shade down, and got back in next to Kit. The New Hampshire morning was chilly and she snuggled down comfortably under the covers. He was still asleep and she curled up against his wide, warm back, closed her eyes and dozed.

Half an hour later he stirred and rolled over. She propped her cheek on her hand and looked down into his face. He gave her a sleepy smile and yawned. "What time is it?" he asked.

"Nine-thirty," she replied. "I feel very decadent."

"You haven't started to be decadent yet, sweetheart," he said with slow amusement.

She tried to look severe. "Everyone will be looking for you."

"Let them look," he murmured. "Kiss me." His voice was very deep and she seemed to feel it in her bones. She bent her head to him. His mouth was gentle under hers; their kiss was infinitely tender. He made no move to touch her. She raised her head and looked down into dark dark eyes. As she stayed where she was suspended over him, he slowly raised his hand to touch her hair. "It's like silk," he murmured. "All of you is like that. Silky and soft . . ." His eyes narrowed and they stared at each other.

Beyond his fingers tangled in her hair he had not touched her. Her body was crying out for him but she too deliberately held herself back, their denial feeding their desire as effectively as any caress could have done. "Take your pajamas off," he said and her hands moved, shaking, to obey him. Their eyes never separated as they both slowly divested themselves of their nightwear. "Now lie down next to me," he directed and she did as he asked, stretching out beside him, her beautiful body positioned for his love.

His hand slid across her stomach and cupped her breast. "Do you want me to wait?" he whispered.

"No." she whispered back, her body on fire for him. "I want you now." She arched up toward him and he came into her hard, his hands gripping her so strongly that he bruised her skin. But she did not object, clinging to him tightly herself, her mouth crushed under his, her whole body shuddering with the pleasure he was giving to her.

They finally lay quietly, breathing hard and still linked together. It was a long time before she found the composure to say, "Now *that* was decadent."

"Um," he answered. "Did you like it?"

"Wow," she said simply, and he chuckled.

"Stick around awhile and we'll try it again. Maybe we can improve."

"I'm always interested in improvement," she replied and he kissed her throat.

"I'm glad to hear that."

They stayed in bed until noon, at which time hunger forced them to get up. "I tell you what," said Kit, yawning and stretching, "I'll go into town and get coffee and donuts and the papers. We can eat here."

"That sounds great." She was watching in admiration as his muscles bunched when he stretched. "I have to get to Mass yet," she added, "but they have one at five this afternoon."

"Well," he conceded slowly, "I might be ready to let you leave by then."

She laughed, got out of bed and bent to pick up her pajamas. "I'm getting dressed," she said firmly. "You lecher."

He grinned. "I have a lot of time to make up for." He watched her folding her pajamas to put them in the drawer. "You always did wear the sexiest nightwear," he murmured. "Flannel pajamas."

"When you live in New England you opt for warmth," she replied serenely, putting them away. "I never could see the point of a sexy nightgown anyway. I bought one for our honeymoon, you remember, and all it did was wind up on the floor."

His teeth were very white in his dark face. "True." He headed for the shower. "I won't be long."

She put on her terry-cloth robe and went out into the living room to finish tidying up. It was a good thing the maids didn't work on Sunday, she thought as she poured herself a glass of apple juice. They would have gotten a shock if they had opened the bedroom door half an hour ago!

Kit came out of the bedroom wearing navy cotton pants and a red-striped rugby shirt. "I'll be back shortly," he said. "Don't run away."

"I won't. But neither do I think I'll accompany you out to the porch."

He laughed. "No use borrowing trouble," he agreed. After he had left, Mary went in to take a shower.

He was gone for almost an hour and she was on the point of having more peanut butter and jelly for breakfast when she heard his car pull up in front of the cottage. He came in carrying a bag in either hand. "Coffee," he said, putting one bag down on the table. "Donuts." He put down the other bag.

"Thank heavens," Mary replied, taking out a container of coffee. "I was about to have a caffeine fit."

He sat down next to her on the sofa and picked up his own coffee. "I ran into George as I was driving out, that's what kept me."

"Oh? What did he have to say?" She sipped her coffee with obvious pleasure.

"He gave me this." Kit reached into his pocket and pulled out a folded sheet of paper. "It's John Calder's review, the one that will appear in the *Times* tomorrow morning. He dropped a copy of it off with George before he left this morning."

Mary put her coffee down and took the papers from him. There was more than one typed sheet and she spread them out and began to read. The first sentence allayed her anxiety: "A milestone in American theater occurred last night with the Yarborough Festival's production of *Hamlet* with (with the single exception of Melvin Shaw's Polonius) an all-American cast." She glanced up at Kit quickly but he was calmly munching a donut. She looked down and continued to read. There was praise for George, for his "sensitive and perceptive" handling of the staging and the relationships among the characters. Carolyn was singled out for her "bewildered and delicate Ophelia," Frank for his "simple, gullible, likeable Laertes," and Alfred for his "authoritative Claudius." Calder devoted a whole paragraph to Margot's "light-minded, light-hearted, light-skirted Gertrude."

The second half of the article concentrated on Kit. "If anyone had doubts about the acting ability of Christopher Douglas," she read, "they were laid to rest last night." Mary went through the remainder of the article in growing jubilation. When she had finished she looked back to the one sentence that had lodged in her mind and read it out loud: "Quite possibly the finest Shakespearean performance ever delivered by an American actor." She put the article down and turned to him with glowing eyes. "Oh, Kit!"

"Nice, huh?" he said nonchalantly.

"Nice? It's marvelous. And it's true. You were—oh, I can't find the right word. But I cried and you know I don't often do that."

He put down the dregs of his coffee and looked at her with warm, dark eyes. "Did you cry, Princess? That's the biggest compliment of all." She smiled at him a little mistily. He smiled back and said, "I'm afraid I've eaten all the donuts."

"You haven't!" She leaned forward and grabbed the

bag. There was one left and she appropriated it firmly. "I imagine George was thrilled," she said around a mouthful.

"He was feeling pretty good. He's sure we can go to Broadway if I want to."

"Do you?"

"What do you want to do?" he returned. "Would you like living in New York for a few months."

"Sure," she said recklessly. "I could always work at the Columbia library if I wanted to."

His brow cleared. "In that case, I'll do it. It will help enormously, when I try to borrow money to do a picture of my own, if people are reassured that I really *can* act."

"Do you know," she said thoughtfully, "Daddy might lend us some money. He's always looking for a good investment."

"Yes, well I haven't worked out the details yet. But I will. I have no intention of overspending my own budget."

She smiled a little abstractedly. "Speaking of Daddy, I think I'd better call home and break the news."

"Mel flew in this morning," he said in a seeming non sequitur. "He and George have set up a press conference for this afternoon at three. The TV people will be there. I said I'd come."

"Then I most certainly better call home," she said decisively.

"You don't mind if I announce that we're back together?"

She leaned over and kissed his cheek. "I'll come with you." She picked up the phone. "But first . . ."

He sat quietly next to her as she dialed the familiar number. Her mother answered on the third ring. "Hi Mother," she said.

"Mary Kate! Darling, how are you?"

"Fine. Listen, Mom, sit down. I have some news that may surprise you. Are you sitting?"

"Yes," came the faint response.

"Kit and I are getting back together again."

"Oh, Mary Kate, I'm so glad!" was the surprising reply. "I've been praying all month that this would happen."

Mary stared at the receiver. "You have?"

"Yes. And your father too. Is Kit there?"

"Yes."

"Put him on. I want to talk to him."

"Okay." Mary held out the phone to him. "She wants to talk to you."

Kit looked a little warily at the receiver. He took the phone in a distinctly apprehensive manner and she smiled to herself. He had always been a little nervous around her mother. "It isn't that I don't like her," he had once said to Mary. "I do. It's just that she's so proper. Every time she looks at me, I'm sure I'm eating with the wrong fork or something." He said now into the phone, "Hello Julia, how are you?"

Mary couldn't hear her mother's response, but from the expression on Kit's face she gathered that it was satisfactory. "I wasn't sure how you would feel about it," he said. There was silence as he listened to the voice on the other end and then he grinned. "Yes, well I've been chasing her mercilessly for three weeks and she's finally given in." Silence. "I feel the same way," he said. "Okay, fine, I'd love to talk to him." Pause.

"Hi Bob. Yes. Well, I'm happy about it too. Oh, the play went well. Looks like we'll be going to Broadway." Long long pause. "Thank you very much," said Kit quietly. Then, "I'll put your daughter on."

She took the receiver. "Hi, Daddy."

"I'm so happy for you, Mary Kate."

"Me too." She laughed a little. "I don't think I realized how *un*happy I've been all these years."

"Well, your mother and I did, honey, and that's why we're so pleased you and Kit have decided to try it again. I always thought you had something special."

"We did. We do."

"Great. When can we expect to see you?"

"Hold on a minute." She put her hand over the phone and said to Kit, "Do you want to stop off and see my folks after you've finished here?"

"Sure," he said.

"Daddy? Kit is tied up here until the end of August, but we'll come for a weekend after that. Yes, the play was terrific. Kit was fantastic. The rave reviews should start on the TV news tonight. Okay. That would be lovely. How about next weekend? Good. We'll see you then. Bye now."

She hung up the phone. "They're coming up to see the play next weekend."

"Great. Better book them into the Stafford Inn."

"Yes. What time did you say the press conference started?"

"Three o'clock." He looked at his watch. "Half an hour from now. God, where did the day go?"

"If you can't remember," she said dryly, "I'll be very insulted."

"You'll have to remind me," he murmured. "Tonight."

"You're insatiable." She stood up and brushed donut crumbs off her lap. He leered. "*And* a donut thief," she added. "What does one wear to a press conference anyway?"

"I'm wearing exactly what I've got on," he replied equably.

She looked at him critically. "You might shave."

"I might do that," he conceded.

She looked down at her jeans and bare feet. "I have to change, that's for sure." He didn't move. "Well, come on," she urged, "don't just sit there staring at me! Do you have your razor here?"

"No."

"Well then go and get it. Or better still, shave over there. I could use the bathroom." And she shoved him out the door.

The rec room was crowded with people, television cameras, and still-photographers when Mary and Kit walked in together. George was talking with a network television critic when he looked up and saw them. It seemed the whole room made the discovery at the same time, for suddenly cameras began to flash and TV equipment to roll. Mary looked startled and George watched as Kit put a protective arm around her shoulders. He felt a deep pain around the region of his heart as he looked at the pair in front of the fireplace.

They made a striking couple, both tall and slim and black-haired, Kit's bronzed masculinity a foil for the magnolia creaminess of his wife. Mary had regained her poise and was smiling a little. She looked cool and composed, as if she had done this sort of thing every day of her life. Kit had dropped his arm but the impression of unity they gave off was very strong.

So she had gone back to him, George thought dully. He really wasn't all that surprised. How could he—or any man—hope to compete with Chris Douglas? The hell of it was, thought George as he moved closer to the fireplace, he liked Chris. He would like him much better, however, if he wasn't married to Mary.

"Yes," he heard Chris saying in response to a question, "I'd accept an offer to go to Broadway. But only if my coworkers—including Mr. Moore and Miss Nash—are invited as well."

George looked quickly across the room to where Carolyn and Frank were standing together. The expressions on their faces brought a reluctant grin to his own. Yes, it was very difficult to dislike Chris Douglas.

Mary was talking now. "I'm not quite sure what my future teaching plans will be," she answered a woman reporter's question. "So much depends on my husband's schedule." She sounded sweet and demure and George saw Kit give her a quick, amused look.

There was another question and then Kit was signaling to George to come and join them. As he came slowly forward Mary turned the blue of her eye on his face. He smiled a little crookedly at what he saw there. A reporter asked him a question and he turned to answer it.

At four-fifteen Kit called a halt. He and Mary made a gracious but determined exit, and as they were walk-

ing back up through the pines she heaved a sigh of relief.

"I know," he said. "But I do that sort of thing very
seldom."

"Why did you do it today?" she asked curiously.

"I thought it would help George and the festival."

She leaned her head against his arm for a minute.
"I have to get moving to church."

"I'll come with you," he said.

She stopped and stared at him. The only time he
had ever gone to church with her was the day they
were married. "You don't have to," she said faintly.

"I'd like to. I've done a lot of thinking in the last
four years and that was one of the things I thought
about."

"Oh, darling." Her face was radiant. "It would
make me so happy."

He took her hand and began to walk again up the
hill. "Well, that's what I want to do," he said. "Make
you happy."

She raised their linked hands and kissed his fingers.
"You do. You do."

RAPTURE ROMANCE

Provocative and sensual, passionate and tender— the magic and mystery of love in all its many guises

RAPTURE ROMANCE

Provocative and sensual,
passionate and tender—
the magic and mystery of love
in all its many guises

Coming next month

CRYSTAL DREAMS
by Diana Morgan

They met when her car skidded on ice: Mariette, an intellectual Bostonian striving for her Ph.D., and Bull, a rough and tumble hockey pro. Worlds apart, but in one unforgettable moment of passion they found a private world all their own—until shocking newspaper headlines trumpeted Bull's name and shattered Mariette's dreams. . . .

THE WINE-DARK SEA
by Ellie Winslow

"I wouldn't go to bed with you if you were the last man in Greece . . ." From the start of the Greek tour, Lydia had disliked Nick Aristou's arrogant ways. Neither his darkly handsome looks nor the fact that he was buying the tourist cruise business she worked for gave him the right to assume she was "company property". But she couldn't deny the waves of desire his slightest touch awoke in her. . . .

Fabulous Fiction from SIGNET

(0451)

☐ **RETURN TO YESTERDAY** by June Lund Shiplett.
(121228—$3.50)*

☐ **JOURNEY TO YESTERDAY** by June Lund Shiplett.
(121260—$3.50)*

☐ **THUNDER IN THE WIND** by June Lund Shiplett.
(119959—$3.50)*

☐ **DEFY THE SAVAGE WINDS** by June Lund Shiplett.
(093372—$2.50)*

☐ **HOLD BACK THE SUN** by June Lund Shiplett.
(110153—$2.95)*

☐ **RAGING WINDS OF HEAVEN** by June Lund Shiplett.
(094395—$2.50)

☐ **REAP THE BITTER WINDS** by June Lund Shiplett.
(116909—$2.95)*

☐ **THE WILD STORMS OF HEAVEN** by June Lund Shiplett.
(112474—$2.95)*

☐ **GLYNDA** by Susannah Leigh. (085485—$2.50)*

☐ **WINE OF THE DREAMERS** by Susannah Leigh.
(091574—$2.95)

☐ **YESTERDAY'S TEARS** by Susannah Leigh. (117646—$3.50)*

☐ **BANNERS OF SILK** by Rosiland Laker. (115457—$3.50)*

☐ **CLAUDINE'S DAUGHTER** by Rosiland Laker.
(091590—$2.25)*

☐ **WARWYCK'S WOMAN** by Rosiland Laker. (088131—$2.25)*

☐ **PORTRAIT IN PASSION** by Maggie Osborne.
(111079—$3.50)*

☐ **SALEM'S DAUGHTER** by Maggie Osborne. (096029—$2.75)*

☐ **YANKEE PRINCESS** by Maggie Osborne. (118200—$3.50)*

*Prices slightly higher in Canada

Buy them at your local bookstore or use this convenient coupon for ordering.
THE NEW AMERICAN LIBRARY, INC.,
P.O. Box 999, Bergenfield, New Jersey 07621
Please send me the books I have checked above. I am enclosing $_____
(please add $1.00 to this order to cover postage and handling). Send check
or money order—no cash or C.O.D.'s. Prices and numbers are subject to change
without notice.
Name_____
Address_____
City _____ State _____ Zip Code _____
Allow 4-6 weeks for delivery.
This offer is subject to withdrawal without notice.

Big Bestsellers from SIGNET

RAPTURE ROMANCE—*Reader's Opinion Questionnaire*

Thank you for filling out our questionnaire. Your response to the following questions will help us to bring you more and better books, by telling us what you are like, what you look for in a romance, and how we can best keep you informed about our books. Your opinions are important to us, and we appreciate your help.

1. What made you choose this particular book? (This book is #_____)
   Art on the front cover_____
   Plot descriptions on the back cover_____
   Friend's recommendation_____
   Other (please specify)_____
2. Would you rate this book:
   Excellent_____
   Very good_____
   Good_____
   Fair_____
3. Were the love scenes (circle answers):
   A. Too explicit   Not explicit enough   Just right
   B. Too frequent   Not frequent enough   Just right
4. How many Rapture Romances have you read?_____
5. Number, from most favorite to least favorite, romance lines you enjoy:
   Adventures in Love_____
   Ballantine Love and Life_____
   Bantam Circle of Love_____
   Dell Candlelight _____
   Dell Candlelight Ecstasy_____
   Jove Second Chance at Love_____
   Harlequin_____
   Harlequin Presents_____
   Harlequin Super Romance_____
   Rapture Romance_____
   Silhouette_____
   Silhouette Desire_____
   Silhouette Special Edition_____
6. Please check the *types* of romances you enjoy:
   Historical romance_____
   Regency romance_____
   Romantic suspense_____
   Short, light contemporary romance_____
   Short, sensual contemporary romance_____
   Longer contemporary romance_____
7. What is the age of the oldest _____ youngest _____ heroine you would like to read about? The oldest _____ youngest _____ hero?

8. What elements do you dislike in a romance?
   Mystery/suspense_____
   Supernatural_____
   Other (please specify) _____
9. We would like to know:
   - How much television you watch
     Over 4 hours a day_____
     2–4 hours a day_____
     0–2 hours a day_____
   - What your favorite programs are
     _____
     _____

   - When you usually watch television
     8 a.m. to 5 p.m._____
     5 p.m. to 11 p.m._____
     11 p.m. to 2 a.m._____
10. How many magazines do you read regularly?
    More than 6_____
    3–6_____
    0–3_____
    Which of these are your favorites?
    _____
    _____

To get a picture of our readers, and to know where to reach them, the following personal information will be most helpful, if you don't mind giving it, and will be kept only for our records.

Name _____
Address_____
City _____
State_____ Zip code_____

Please check your age group:
17 and under_____
18–34_____
35–49_____
50–64_____
64 and older_____

Education:
  Now in high school_____
  Now in college_____
  Graduated from high school_____
  Completed some college_____
  Graduated from college_____

Are you now working outside the home?
  Yes_____ No_____
  Full time_____
  Part time_____
  Job title_____

Thank you for your time and effort. Please send the completed questionnaire and answer sheet to: Robin Grunder, RAPTURE ROMANCE, New American Library, 1633 Broadway, New York, NY 10019